A NICE DAY FOR SPACE INVADING

It was sixteen o'clock on the third Valoonaday in the month of Green, and Hex (or Hex-37, to give him his full name) was huddled under his duvet, tinkering away at his latest robot creation.

"Primary control module looking good . . . limbs responsive – let's see if he ticks," Hex said. He flicked a small switch and then closed the control panel on the back of the robot's head. As he held it in one of his suckers, the small, round robot hummed and buzzed into life – blinking with confusion.

"Well, hello there," said Hex.

"Chik-POP!" said the little robot.

"Sorry, I still haven't worked out how to make you talk properly," said Hex, as the robot spun its tiny arms around. "But don't worry, I've always spoken pretty good 'robot'."

"Chik-POP!" said the robot, happily.

"That's just what I was going to say! You know, I think you might be my best robot yet," said Hex, proudly. "I'm going to call you Glitch. My name is He-EEEEEYOW!"

A long metal pincer grabbed Hex by the ankle, lifting him out of his slumber pod.

"YOoOW! Knock it off, T.K., I'm awake, I'm awake!" screeched Hex.

"Another beautiful day on Planet X! The suns are shining, the air is very nearly non-toxic, and there's only a 32.4 per cent chance of meteor showers!" said T.K.421, the computer that ran Hex's fully automated floating home high in the skies of Planet X.

The pincer dropped Hex on to the floor and then

snaked back into the wall. Hex picked up his little robot and checked that it wasn't broken.

"Are you OK, Glitch?"

"POP-glik!" said Glitch, his head spinning around.

"Why, you've made a little robot! How clever," said T.K. "Not as clever as me, of course, but then I am a T.K.4 model – the cleverest home computers since the T.K.3! No other home computer is more dedicated to making a comfortable environment for the modern space invader! So what does your little robot do? Shoot death rays? Launch mutation spores?"

"He doesn't do anything. I just made him for fun," said Hex. There was a pause. Finally, T.K. replied, "Does not compute – 'fun' is not a function."

"It's not supposed to. . . I'll explain later," Hex sighed. "I'd better get ready for school."

"Absolutely! It's your first day at Sporg's School for Space Invaders!" said T.K.421, excitedly. "Oh, Master Hex, your father would be *so* proud to see you start your training! If he wasn't lost somewhere in deep space, that is."

3

"Thanks for reminding me, T.K.," Hex grumbled. He stretched his antenna, and stepped lazily on to the conveyor-floor. "Cleansing zone, please."

"Faster than a hypersaucer hopping to light speed, Master Hex!" said T.K. and the conveyor-floor whisked Hex out of his room, down the hall and into the cleansing zone so fast that he could barely stay on his feet. As a cleansing tube lowered around him, Hex looked at his image in the reflector. Apart from looking tired (his telepathy nodes were *particularly* swollen), Hex was bright green with two large, round eyes and a bulbous head. Out of the top of his head grew a long, single antenna. He rubbed his eyes with his suckers and yawned out of his gills.

"Just give me the basic rinse," he mumbled, as T.K.'s cleansing programme whirred into action.

SKOOSH! CHUNG! ZWORT! VWASH! SKWETCH!

"YoOOooOOW! Oo! *Ow!* Uff! GAH!" cried Hex, as the cleansing tube sprayed, rubbed and scrubbed.

"You can't very well start space invader school without polished eyeballs and scrubbed suckers, now can you?" said T.K. eagerly as Hex was conveyed into the clothing zone. "Arms up!" said T.K. as more robotic pincers shot out of the wall, holding various items of clothing.

Two point nine seconds later, Hex was dressed. He was wearing a shiny, silvery uniform, large magna-boots and a brand new tele-belt. Hex made sure the belt was set to OFF (he didn't want it accidentally picking up a teleportation signal and transporting him who knows where) and then slipped Glitch into his pocket just as he was delivered into the ingestion zone. "You're 3.5 seconds late for breakfast, Hex-37," said Hex's mother as she swept into the ingestion zone. She straightened his antenna as she passed by and sat down. The light of the suns shone through the window into her huge, translucent brain-sack, illuminating her pulsating brain. "You know what they say," she continued, "laziness leads to lateness, lateness leads to disintegration."

"Yes, Mum," sighed Hex, as a bowl of grey gloop was plonked on to the table in front of him. He stared at it and scrunched up his face. "Gloop again for breakfast, then?"

"You know what they say – a bowl of gloop a day keeps the medical droid away," said his mother. Gloop was the only food on Planet X. All other foods had been "gloopified" to become an ingredient in gloop. Gloop tasted sort of like everything, which meant it sort of tasted like nothing, and Hex hated it.

"Scoop that gloop! It's got everything a space invader needs!" said T.K., as a spoon arm extended from the wall and slopped more gloop into Hex's bowl.

"Today is a big day for you, Hex," said his mother. "You could work hard at your training and be a great space invader, like me. Or you could be lazy and end up lost in space, like your father."

Hex sighed. His mother always insisted that Hex's dad was just lazy, as he had never managed to graduate from space invader school. But Hex knew different. He knew that his dad was the victim of a terrible family curse – the "Hex Effect". The Hex Effect followed one general rule: once any male Hex started space invading training, everything went horribly, horribly wrong. There was nothing they could do about it. Hex's dad had it, as did his dad before him, and so on, for thirty-six generations. In fact, the Hexes were the only planetexians in history never to have done any actual invading:

- Hex-36 – Sucked into a black hole during hypersaucer training

- Hex-35 – Teleported into deep space during tele-belt training

- Hex-34 – Permanently transmogrified into a six-bellied skweech during mutation ray class

Hex-33 – Disintegrated on the toilet (no one really knows how)

Not surprisingly, Hex was more than a bit concerned about starting space invader school. In fact, he could think of nothing worse. Unfortunately, on Planet X, space invading was all anyone ever seemed to care about.

"Do I *really* have to go?" asked Hex, failing to notice Glitch climb out of his pocket and clamber down the chair to the floor.

"Of course you have to go! How are you going to learn to be a space invader otherwise?" said his mother, as if the suggestion was completely ridiculous. She paused for a moment, and then rested her suckers on Hex's shoulders. "Listen to me, Hex. You're a very talented boy. There isn't a piece of technology on Planet X that you couldn't take apart and put back together. But you have a *duty* to put your talents to space invading, not wasting them making silly little robots. I mean, if only they had *something* to do with invading . . . you could have built a sentry-bot, like the ones that guard the empress. At least they have ray-guns."

"They're not *supposed* to have anything to do with space invading," said Hex, grumpily. "They're just robots."

"Then there's no point in making them, is there?" continued his mother. "I mean it this time, Hex. It's time that you focus on the important things in life – space and invading. Do I make myself clear?" She began striding around the kitchen, as Glitch zoomed between her legs. "Look around you. Everything we have we got as a result of space invading. Space invading is what we do – it's *all* we do! Planetexians didn't get where we are building useless little toys which do nothing except get underfoot!"

KRUNCH!

Hex looked down. His mother had stepped on Glitch!

"My robot! Glitch, are you OK?" shouted Hex, jumping down from the table and scooping Glitch up. "Talk to me! How many suckers am I holding up?" he added, but Glitch's head fell off and clunked to the floor.

"You see? This is *exactly* what I'm talking about," said his mother. "How do you expect to be a space invader if you're not thinking about space invading?"

"Space invading is stupid!" growled Hex, angrily, as he picked up Glitch's head. "I don't even want to be a space—"

"*Shhhhhh!*" said his mother, slapping a sucker over his mouth. "Do you want to be disintegrated? You know better than to question the will of the empress! Honestly, Hex, what would your father say if he heard you talking like that?"

"Given that he's lost in outer space, I'd be pretty surprised if he can hear me!" said Hex, putting Glitch's crumpled parts back into his pocket.

"Yes, well, perhaps if he'd taken his space invader training seriously, he wouldn't have messed everything up so badly," said his mother. She shook her head and turned on the morning news-vid.

WHERE NEXT FOR PLANET X? LIVE FINAL TODAY!

"The wait is almost over! After months of voting, the final four contenders for invasion have been selected, and tonight, live from the palace, Her Majestic Green, the Empress Valoona XIII, will decide which planet will next be conquered by the planetexian invasion force. The empress, in her infinite and unquestioned wisdom, will make the selection using the traditional method of sticking a pin in a map whilst blindfolded.

"The shortlist for the soon-to-be-renamed PLANET X number 914 (or thereabouts) are:

PLANET ZAXON (odds of 6:1)
PLANET STELA (odds of 5:1)
PLANET INSTA (odds of 20:1)
PLANET EARTH (odds of 100:1)

The decision will be announced this afternoon, at twenty o'clock. Invaders! Place your bets and charge your ray-guns!"

"Wonderful news!" said his mother. "Just think, Hex, if you do well in your training, you might even get fast-tracked to the invasion fleet!"

"Invasion day always comes around so fast," sighed Hex. "I thought we'd just got settled here – on *this* Planet X."

"You know what they say – those who can, invade. Those who can't, get disintegrated," said his mother, her huge, oval eyes glazing over as she recalled her days as a captain of the 101st hypersaucer fleet. She couldn't wait to invade the next planet!

"Only five minutes until the skybus arrives! Time to go!" cried T.K. loudly, shooting a pincer out of the wall and plucking Hex from his seat.

"I'm ready, I'm ready!" said Hex as T.K. dropped him on to the conveyor. His mother rested her sucker on the top of his head.

"I know you'll make me proud, Hex," she said. A moment later she added, "You will, won't you?"

Hex didn't reply. He just waited until he was whisked into the ejection chute and fired on to the waiting platform. He could already see the snake-like skybus stopping at each of the floating homes. He took a deep breath and stared at the two bright suns in the pink planetexian sky as the skybus pulled up at the docking platform.

"All aboard!" said the driver. Hex looked back, to see his mother (and one of T.K.'s robotic hands) waving at him through the window. He weakly waved a sucker, and then got on.

SPORG'S SCHOOL FOR SPACE INVADERS

"Next stop, Sporg's School for Space Invaders," said the skybus driver, and a cheer went up from each of the 118 excited planetexian children. In fact, everyone cheered except Hex. He slinked down the skybus looking for a spare seat.

As he shuffled down the aisle, the other children pressed their faces against the windows as the skybus passed over the emerald palace of Empress Valoona. The palace seemed to shimmer in the morning light, and Hex imagined the empress inside – plotting the invasion of planet after planet. Hex could hardly believe that a matter of years ago, this whole world had been pretty much flattened by the invading planetexian army. No one was allowed to talk about what it used to be called or who used to live here, but everyone seemed to have forgotten anyway. All that mattered was that it had been rebuilt and renamed as *the new* Planet X.

"You can sit next to me if you like!" said a voice. It came from the biggest boy Hex had ever seen. He was a brighter green than Hex, with a huge round belly and head, and stubby little legs. He smiled and eagerly patted the seat next to him.

"Uh, thanks," said Hex, trying to squeeze on to what little seat there was left.

"We're going to be space invasers!" said the giant boy, excitedly. "Can you believe it?"

"Uh, I suppose," said Hex, a little nervous.

"I can't believe they make us wait so long before we start! I've been wanting to blow stuff up since I was an egg!" the boy said, making a ray-gun shape with his suckers. "BOOM! BOOM!"

"M-me too," said Hex, checking to see if there were any other free seats around.

"Great! We can be invasing buddies! I'm Dooper. What's your name?" asked the boy.

"Hex," mumbled Hex.

"Team Dooper and Hex. . ." Dooper mused. "Sounds good! 'Look at Team Dooper and Hex go!' they'll say. 'Did you see that? Team Dooper and Hex invased that whole planet with one sucker tied behind their backs! BOOM! Here's a medal and some extra gloop for Team Dooper and Hex! The best space invasers on Planet X!' That's what they'll say!"

"Yeah, that's what they'll say," said Hex, forcing a smile.

"Actually," said another voice behind him, "I think you'll find that the title of best space invader on Planet X will be going to *me*."

Hex turned around to see a pointy-faced boy stared at him with narrow, black eyes. He was wearing a 3D holo-badge that read INVADER-IN-TRAINING.

"My name is Steek," he said, as if everyone should

already know who he was. Hex and Dooper just looked back blankly. "My father was Steek-55, captain of the 229th hypersaucer fleet, which led the invasion of this Planet X. He said I have what it takes to be the best of the best!"

"Better than Team Dooper and Hex?" said Dooper. "No way! We're going to invase everywhere – twice! Isn't that right, Hex?"

"Uh. . ." began Hex.

"Wait a minute . . . *Hex*? You're Hex? Not Hex-37? 'Hex Effect' Hex?" said Steek, examining him with disdain.

"Do I know you?" asked Hex, wondering how on Planet X this boy knew about the Hex Effect.

"I know *you* – you're Hex-37! Your dad was Hex-36," snarled the boy. "My dad told me to look out for you! He went to Sporg's with your dad. He said that your dad couldn't even go *near* a hypersaucer or a ray-gun without something going wrong. He said you Hexes are bad luck."

"Um. . . Well. . ." Hex began anxiously, wishing he

was the one that was lost in space right now.

"And your dad never even graduated, did he? He was stuck at Sporg's for, like, twenty years?"

Hex took a deep, defeated breath and said, "Twenty two."

"Twenty two? Twenty two years training and he still didn't graduate! By the empress's underpants, he must have been the worst pupil ever!" laughed Steek, but then he fixed Hex with a stern glare. "You'd better stay out of my antenna-range, Hex-37. I'm going to be the greatest space invader in the history of Planet X and the last thing I need is you messing everything up. Understand?"

"I'll be careful," said Hex.

"You'll be dead," said Steek, poking Hex with a sucker.

"Why don't you pick on someone your own size, Stink?" said Dooper.

"It's *Steek*," said Steek, squaring up to Dooper. "And I'd have to eat all the gloop on Planet X to be *your* size. Even your antenna is fat!"

"I am not fat! I have overactive elbow-glands!" said Dooper, shaking his elbows in Steek's face.

"You're so fat it'd take a hundred hypersaucers just to drag you off that seat!" laughed Steek.

"Oh, put a sock in your gills, Steek," said another voice. Hex turned around to see a girl lean over Steek's chair and grab him by the antenna.

"Ow! Get off, Opo!" yelped Steek. "That hurts!"

"Don't listen to my brother, he's just nervous because Dad isn't here to hold his sucker," said Opo.

"I am not! Shut up, Opo!" whined Steek as he sat back in his seat.

"He's your brother?" asked Hex.

"We're twins. He got all the meanness, I got everything else," said Opo with a grin. "Don't worry, he's all talk. And I'm sure you'll be great invaders," she said, and smiled. Hex blushed a deep shade of green and looked out of the window. He hadn't noticed that the skybus had been descending into the city. They had arrived at Sporg's.

"Last stop, everyone off!" said the skybus driver as they landed outside a huge silvery-white building, with dozens of tall, thin spires ending in vast, spherical learning pods. Hex had never been this far into the city before. As he climbed off the skybus, he was struck with how bright and noisy it was. Everywhere he looked, massive floating billboards bellowed their slogans into the air:

Hex didn't have time to stop and stare – the ever-growing sea of children had begun bundling into the school as skybus after skybus dropped off yet more space invaders in training. Hex was dragged along with the crowd, guided by a horde of spindly assisto-bots into the main hall.

"Move along, no dawdling, tuck in those suckers, there's room enough for everyone," said the assisto-bots, shuffling between the crowd on their thin metal legs. After a while, Hex spotted a fat, imposing-looking old planetexian emerging from the end of the hall on a floating podium.

"File in, file in! That's it!" bellowed the fat

planetexian. "I am Sporg-109, but you will call me Headmaster Sporg! Never 'Sporgy'! Only my mother called me Sporgy and I had her disintegrated years ago!"

Dooper yelled, "BOOM!" at the mere mention of disintegration.

"Silence! There shall be no booming in my school unless I say so!" shouted Headmaster Sporg. "As long as there has been space invading, there have been space invader schools! And Sporg's is the best space invader school this side of the space invader school just down the road! Am I right?"

"Yes, Headmaster!" said the assisto-bots.

"Yes, Headmaster!" came the pupils' cry.

"Yes, Headmaster!" yelled Dooper a moment later.

"For those of you returning to Sporg's to continue your five-year training, welcome back!" said Sporg. "I am sure you are all delighted to be back, so that you, too, may become space invaders! After all, what else are you going to do?"

There was confused murmuring from the pupils, as if

they had never even thought about doing anything else. Only Hex had a better idea – he took Glitch out of his pocket and set about repairing him.

"Poor Glitch," whispered Hex, trying to reattach Glitch's head. "Don't worry, I'll fix you properly when we get home. . ."

"Shut your gills, Hex, I'm trying to listen!" said Steek. "You might not give a quark about space invading, but I do!"

"SILENCE!" boomed Headmaster Sporg. "Talking, whispering, mumbling and unwarranted telepathy are punishable by disintegration! Now, where was I – oh yes! Those of you who are new to the school, pin back your hear lobes! Here at Sporg's, over the next five years, you will learn all the skills that you need to be a galaxy-class space invader! But for those of you who think that space invading is all about shooting death rays at stuff, you must think again! Oh dear me no – there are hundreds of different ways to take over a planet and you are going to learn them all. You will learn how to pilot a hypersaucer through meteor showers and black holes! You will learn how to carry out abductions and the proper procedures for probing! You will master mind-control, and become masters of disguise! But most importantly, you will learn how to shoot death rays at stuff! Not straight away, of course. There are a good four and a half years of dull theory tests and dreary essays before we get to the good stuff. This is a school, after all! Now, repeat the school motto: *If in doubt, disintegrate!*"

"If in doubt, disintegrate!" repeated the assisto-bots together.

"If in doubt, disintegrate!" shouted the thousands of children. This time Hex did join in, but only because he could see Opo looking at him.

"Remember that motto, and you will never fail. Which is important, because if you *do* fail, you'll be disintegrated," said Headmaster Sporg. "Now, set your belts to 'receive' and stand by to be teleported to your designated learning pod."

Hex and the other children grabbed the dials on their tele-belts and turned them to receive the teleported beam. A second later, they were bathed in a bright blue light, which transported them instantly from the hall to their learning pods.

Everyone except Hex.

The teleport hadn't worked! Hex looked up at Sporg, who was staring suspiciously at him from the other end of the hall. He frantically turned the dial on his tele-belt as the headmaster floated towards him.

"What's this? Not teleported? Causing trouble already, boy? And in your first . . ." the headmaster checked his watch and tutted – "2.4 minutes at school, oh dear me no. Didn't you check your tele-belt before you left?"

"No; I mean, yes! Sorry, I don't know what's, I mean, it's not. . ." Hex began, desperately turning the dial until it began to smoke. Finally, the dial popped off in his suckers, and Hex shrieked as the belt exploded!

"Yow!" screamed Hex, and as he unclipped his belt and threw it to the floor, one thought burned in his brain-sack.

The Hex Effect had begun.

THE P.A.D.

"Exploded, eh? The first sign of a poorly maintained tele-belt," said Headmaster Sporg, staring at Hex with all three of his eyes.

"No, but . . . it's brand new! My T.K. unit only took it out of the box this morning," said Hex, gathering up the pieces of his ruined tele-belt. He couldn't believe that the Hex Effect had started already!

"SILENCE!" boomed Headmaster Sporg.

"There are no excuses for excuses," tutted an assisto-bot.

"Under normal circumstances I'd just disintegrate you

and be done with it," continued Headmaster Sporg, his brain-sack pulsating. Hex whimpered with fear. "But it is your first day and finding your way to your learning pod on foot might just be punishment enough. There are six hundred and nineteen of them, after all."

"Six hundred and nineteen?" gasped Hex, his wide eyes wider than ever.

"Well, don't just stand there, boy. . ." said the headmaster, his antenna glowing green with rage. "MOVE!!"

Three hours and four minutes of wandering identical-looking corridors later, Hex stumbled across his learning pod, by which time he was wondering why he hadn't just gone home.

"Roswell class," he said, reading the holo-sign on the portal door. Cautiously, he pressed the OPEN button.

"Ah, Hex-37, I assume? How good of you to join us," said the teacher as the portal slid open. "Well don't just stand there like a wingless nudlork, come in, come in." She was a spindly, long-headed planetexian, with a holo-badge that said "Miss Voob".

"Sorry I'm late, I—" began Hex, but Miss Voob just waved him to his desk. He made his way past Dooper, who gave him a suckers-up signal, and Opo, who smiled at him just long enough to make him blush again.

"Not to worry, there's no rush – we're not invading yet!" chuckled Miss Voob. "But what's this? Where's your tele-belt?" continued Miss Voob, pointing at Hex's still smouldering trousers.

"Umm . . . I had a little trouble," said Hex, brushing off the last remnants of the belt from his trousers.

"Well, you must learn to walk before you can teleport, as they say," said Miss Voob. "Then again, we can't have you wandering around the school on foot – you'll wear out your magna-boots! I'm sure there's a spare tele-belt in the lost property box."

Hex waited awkwardly as a large, dusty crate materialized on Miss Voob's desk. She dug both suckers in and fished around, finally pulling out an enormous, ancient tele-belt with both hands. It looked like it belonged in a museum and as Miss Voob handed it to Hex, the class began to snigger.

"Here we are. It looks to be a good few years older than you are, but not to worry. Not sure what happened to the previous owner . . . disintegration, I presume. Still, it'll do for now!" said Miss Voob.

As Hex fixed the massive, outdated tele-belt to his trousers, he felt the whole class stare at him and remembered exactly why he hadn't wanted to come to space invader school in the first place.

"Hey, Hex-37! Why are you wearing your grandma's belt?" shouted Steek, and the class burst into laughter.

"I'd be careful with that," said Opo as Hex settled in his seat. "Those old tele-belts have a habit of sending you wherever they please – you could re-materialize anywhere on Planet X! And who knows how long it'd take to pick up the school's teleporter signal after that."

"Great, thanks for the tip," muttered Hex, nervously. At least he might have a chance to try and repair it when he got home. He'd never taken a tele-belt apart before, but he had a fairly good idea of how it worked.

"Settle down, class!" said Miss Voob. "The time has

come for you to receive the most important piece of equipment you will ever need in your invader training. Children, I present to you . . . your P.A.D.s."

Hex watched a small, silver object materialize on his desk. It fitted perfectly into his palm, and had a small screen on the front and a single green button. Hex had seen P.A.D.s before – every grown-up planetexian had one – but he'd never actually used one. Despite himself, he got rather excited about the prospect of having one.

"Look after your Personal Advice Device! This nifty little device will serve as your guide and companion in the days, months and years that follow," said Miss Voob. "Just ask it a question and it will tell you everything you need to know. Now, let's get started! Press the green button to imprint the P.A.D. with your greenetic code. Once you've turned it on, follow the instructions on the screen."

Hex reached out an excited sucker and pressed the button. The P.A.D. played a little jingle and then lit up.

WELCOME TO YOUR PERSONAL ADVICE DEVICE
SET-UP WIZARD. THIS WIZARD WILL GUIDE
YOU THROUGH HOW TO PREPARE YOUR P.A.D.
FOR USE. DEPENDING ON THE SPEED OF YOUR
CONNECTION, THE WIZARD MAY TAKE A FEW
MINUTES TO COMPLETE.
YOUR PROGRESS THROUGH THE SET-UP WIZARD
WILL BE SHOWN ON THE DISINTEGRATING
PLANETEXIAN BAR ON THE LEFT. ONCE THE
PLANETEXIAN IS FULLY DISINTEGRATED,
YOUR P.A.D. IS READY TO USE!

CLICK OK TO CONTINUE.

It all seemed fairly simple. Hex reached out a sucker and clicked OK.

134;P 92E8F# 3RY 9P3##4981U304T 813!!
RECEIVING / DECODING . . . PLEASE WAIT. . .

Hex waited. Then waited a bit longer. He looked around. Everyone else already seemed asking their P.A.D.s questions and getting answers! Then, finally:

SIGNAL CANNOT BE DECODED.
UNKNOWN ERROR HAS OCCURRED.
PERMANENT FATAL ERROR X.
P. A. D. WILL NOW SHUT DOWN.

Suddenly, the screen went black.

"What? No, wait, come back!" cried Hex, staring at the screen. It could only mean one thing – the Hex Effect had returned!

"Is that Master Hex I can hear, shrieking like a Yoopie? Not having more trouble, are you?" said Miss Voob. Hex's unconvincing "Umm . . . no, Miss Voob", was drowned out by the children all laughing at him.

"Oh dear, oh dear. I do hope you haven't broken your P.A.D.," said Miss Voob. "I don't have any replacements and you know the punishment for destruction of planetexian property."

"DISINTEGRATION!" shouted the children together.

"What? *Really?*" said Hex, wishing he'd paid more attention to all those public service vid-announcements on "How to be a Good Citizen (And Not Get

Disintegrated)". "But I didn't break it! I just did what it told me! It must be a faulty dynamizing chip – it's not my fault!" protested Hex, but Miss Voob was already striding towards him. He hid the P.A.D. behind his back, pressing the green button over and over. He chewed nervously on a sucker as Miss Voob loomed over him.

"Well?" she said, sternly.

"Yes, I'm quite well, thank you," said Hex, meekly. "How are you?"

"Oh, I'm fine, thanks for – now hang on! I didn't walk all the way over here for a chat! Hex-37, show me your P.A.D. this minute."

"But I didn't, I mean it wasn't, I mean. . ." he said in a very small voice, and brought his P.A.D. from behind his back. As he held it up, he caught sight of Steek, grinning and making a sucker-to-the-head sign (the universal symbol for "You're *so* going to get disintegrated"). Hex screwed his eyes up in horrible anticipation.

"Well, that all seems in order," said Miss Voob. "Don't

forget to write your name on the back in permanent marker."

Hex opened an eye and peered at his P.A.D.

```
REBOOT SUCCESSFUL
THE SET-UP IS COMPLETE. YOUR P.A.D.
IS NOW READY TO USE.
HAVE A NICE DAY!
```

"How did. . ." he began, then caught sight of Steek looking disappointed. Hex couldn't help but smile. He may not have escaped the Hex Effect, but it was almost worth it to wipe the smirk off Steek's face.

EVERYTHING YOU WANTED TO KNOW ABOUT SPACE INVADING (BUT WERE AFRAID TO ASK)

"Hey . . . hey, Hex!" shouted Dooper, in his best whisper, as Miss Voob explained the lesson-plan for the entire year. "There's a quiz on my P.A.D.! It says I'm going to be the best space invaser ever!"

"Masters Dooper and Hex! Don't make me disintegrate you!" said Miss Voob. "Unless I'm wasting my gill-breath and you *already know* what you're going to be learning in week thirty nine of your training?"

"Umm. . ." said Dooper, looking around as if the answer might appear in the air. Hex used the distraction to inspect his P.A.D. He whispered the word "Quiz" as quietly as he could, and the P.A.D. pinged into life once more.

IT LOOKS LIKE YOU ARE TRYING TO TAKE A QUIZ. CAN I HELP?

CLICK YES TO CONTINUE.

Hex clicked YES.

WELCOME TO THE PLANET X QUIZ! THIS QUIZ WILL TELL YOU EXACTLY HOW SUITED YOU ARE TO SPACE INVADING AND WHETHER YOU ARE LIKELY TO MAKE IT THROUGH YOUR FIRST INVASION INTACT. NOW LET'S BEGIN:

QUESTION 1. IT IS THE END OF THE DAY AND YOU ARE ALL TUCKED UP IN YOUR SLUMBER POD. YOU NOD OFF, LOOKING FORWARD TO ANOTHER DAY OF SPACE-INVASION-RELATED EXCITEMENT. DO YOU DREAM OF:

A)   SPACE INVADING
B)   SPACE-INVASION-RELATED ACTIVITIES,
     SUCH AS DEATH RAY TARGET PRACTICE
C)   BEING DISINTEGRATED
D)   NONE OF THE ABOVE

Hex sighed and pressed "d". He often dreamed of far off worlds, but not once had he dreamed of blowing them up with a death ray. What was the point of travelling all that way just to blow something up?

QUESTION 2. ON A SCHOOL TRIP TO THE PLANET X OBSERVATORY, YOU CATCH SIGHT OF A BRAND NEW PLANET. DO YOU:
A)   REPORT IT IMMEDIATELY TO PLANET X
     HIGH COMMAND (OR A TEACHER) SO THAT
     IT CAN BE ADDED TO THE INVASION LIST
B)   TRAIN A LONG-RANGE DEATH RAY ON IT
     AND BLAST IT FROM A SAFE DISTANCE
C)   DO NOTHING, AND RISK DISINTEGRATION
D)   NONE OF THE ABOVE

Hex was already starting to see a pattern emerge, and he didn't like where things were heading. He pressed "d" again and moved on.

QUESTION 3. WHEN YOU GROW UP, DO YOU WANT TO BE:
A) A SPACE INVADER
B) AN INVADER OF SPACE
C) DISINTEGRATED
D) NONE OF THE ABOVE

Hex shook his head. The quiz wasn't getting him anywhere! He skipped the question and went straight to the results.

IF YOU MAINLY ANSWERED A) YOU ARE A GREAT SPACE INVADER, DEDICATED TO THE CONQUEST OF ALL PLANETS IN THE NAME OF HER MAJESTIC GREEN, THE EMPRESS VALOONA XIII.
IF YOU MAINLY ANSWERED B) YOU HAVE POTENTIAL, BUT THERE IS STILL WORK TO BE DONE. REPORT TO YOUR NEAREST CONDITIONING ZONE FOR EXTRA TRAINING.

IF YOU MAINLY ANSWERED C) YOU WILL BE
DISINTEGRATED.
IF YOU MAINLY ANSWERED D) YOU WILL BE
DISINTEGRATED.

DO YOU WANT TO SAVE YOUR RESULTS?
YES/NO

Hex quickly pressed NO. The last thing he needed was another reason to be disintegrated.

"So, how did you do?" said Opo, leaning towards him. "Do you have what it takes to be a space invader?"

"Uh ... sure! Yeah, straight As all round. I'm all about the invading! There isn't a minute that goes by that I don't think about blowing stuff up!" said Hex, suddenly rather eager to fit in.

"That's right! Team Dooper and Hex!" shouted Dooper.

"That's nothing – look at *this*," said Steek, flashing his P.A.D. in Hex's face. "My P.A.D. just told me I'm going to be the greatest space invader since

Zom-2, inventor of the anti-death-ray death-ray!" boasted Steek.

"Really? Did you mention that you still wet your slumber pod?" said Opo.

"I do not! Shut up, Opo!" screeched Steek.

"You lot! *Please* stop dawdling and switch your tele-belts to 'receive'. Didn't you hear the lunch signal?" said Miss Voob, impatiently. "There's only so much gloop in the Big Gloop Bowl to go around."

Hex looked around. He'd been so engrossed in the one-answer-fits-all quiz that he hadn't even noticed the rest of the class had already teleported.

"See you there!" said Dooper, as he set his tele-belt to "receive". Hex took a deep breath, and reluctantly activated his tele-belt, which rumbled and spluttered like a dying gawker-bird. As he began to de-materialize, Hex crossed his suckers. . .

GLOOPED

Hex felt himself re-materialize and nervously opened his eyes. One thing was certain – he wasn't in the ingestion zone. He was inside a large metal cylinder with a hole in the top and a pipe leading upwards. He looked up through the hole, but it was too dark. Where had his belt sent him? Didn't Opo mention something about re-materializing *anywhere* on Planet X? It didn't take long before Hex started to panic.

"Help! Is anyone out there? I'm stuck in a . . . someplace!" he began, but his cries were quickly drowned out by a loud, rumbling sound coming from above him. Hex looked up again.

"*What is that?*" he whispered to himself. A second and a half later, a tidal wave of gloop cascaded on top of him!

"*Gl-mmUm-FFffpH!*" grunted Hex as gloop poured into the cylinder. Hex tried desperately to swim through the flood of foodstuff, but it was hopeless! The gloop kept coming, until the cylinder was full. Hex held his breath as best he could, but gloop filled his gills, his hear-holes, even his belly-nostril! He was about to pass out when, through the sea of gloop, he heard a strange noise.

VWEEEEEEE — CHUNG!

Suddenly, Hex felt himself moving . . . no, falling! The bottom of the cylinder opened up, and the gloop (and Hex) plummeted downwards!

S L O O o o o o o o o O O O O O R R R R T !

Hex splash-landed into a huge bowl, and the gloop landed on top of him! He scrambled and spluttered his way to the surface of the gloop and grabbed on to the side of the bowl.

"AAAH! Gloop monster!" shrieked Steek, spotting

Hex from halfway down a long table.

Hex wiped the gloop from his eyes and looked around. He was in the ingestion zone . . . inside the Big Gloop Bowl! He slowly realized what had happened – his useless, ancient tele-belt had teleported him inside the gloop tube suspended above the bowl and the tube had squeezed him out, along with five hundred gallons of grey goo! The bowl rested in the centre of an impossibly long table, with the thousands of pupils sitting around it. Every one of them turned to look at Hex.

"Oh no. . ." Hex mumbled through a mouthful of gloop. The Hex Effect was in full swing and he was only halfway through his first day. To make matters worse, he was surrounded by a hundred flying ladle-bots that were zooming around the gloop bowl, spooning out the gloop and carrying it to the children.

"Ow! Yowch! Geddof!" said Hex as the ladle-bots banged into him, or tried to scoop him up in their tiny spoon-arms. A wave of laughter began with the children closest to the Big Gloop Bowl, and soon spread through

the entire ingestion zone. It was enough to get the attention of Headmaster Sporg.

"What's this? A boy in my gloop? How irregular!" bellowed Headmaster Sporg. "Oh dear me no, this won't do at all! Assisto-bots, bring him to me!"

Hex clambered out of the Big Gloop Bowl as a dozen or so assisto-bots emerged from the far corners of the hall and clanked towards him. Before Hex knew it, the assisto-bots had grabbed him in their pincers. Hex dripped gloop all the way down the long table (splashing a bit on Steek, which was a bonus) as he was dragged to the end and plonked in front of Headmaster Sporg.

"What on Planet X is going on today?" asked Headmaster Sporg, peering at Hex through his third eye. "First I have a pupil with a defective tele-belt, and now this! Is this any way for future space invaders to conduct themselves?"

Hex decided not to mention that he *was* the boy with the defective tele-belt. He was just grateful that the gloop seemed to have disguised his appearance.

"Now, I like a bowl of gloop as much as the next

planetexian, but there's no excuse for greediness! A true space invader would never eat more than his share, for he would be taking food from the collective mouth of the planetexian people! The invasion effort must come first!"

"I wasn't trying to eat the—" began Hex.

"Silence! Listening to your argument will take up precious gloop-eating time!" boomed Headmaster Sporg. "No, there's nothing else for it. An example must be made! Now then, what punishment suits the crime? Oooooh, I know! Disintegration!"

"WHAT?" cried Hex. "But . . . but it wasn't my fault! You can't possibly—"

"Silence! I have spoken!" bellowed Headmaster Sporg, getting to his feet and donning his disintegration hat. "As headmaster of Sporg's School for Space Invaders and Class One Disintegration Decree Deliverer, and in the name of Her Majestic Green, the Empress Valoona, I hereby decree that you – um, gloop-covered boy – shall be forthwith taken from this place to the Disintegration Zone, where you shall be placed into the disintegration pod and blasted to atoms!"

"Wait! You can't!" screamed Hex. "I didn't do anything! Well, apart from the gloop thing, but that wasn't my fault! It's my—"

"Silence! It is too late – nothing can save you now! Assisto-bots, take him away!" yelled Sporg, and the assisto-bots grabbed Hex by his arms once again. Hex couldn't believe his hear-lobes – he hadn't even made it through one day! He would even rather be a space invader than be disintegrated. He was debating whether to try and make a run for it, when:

"ATTENTION CITIZENS OF PLANET X! HER MAJESTIC GREEN, THE EMPRESS VALOONA, IS ABOUT TO ADDRESS HER PEOPLE! CEASE AND DESIST ALL ACTION, INCLUDING INGESTION, INVASION AND DISINTEGRATION!"

The announcement was so loud it shook the walls of the school. The assisto-bots immediately dropped Hex to the floor, and everyone withdrew their feeding tubes from their bowls. A massive holo-screen appeared in the air above them. On the screen was a fat-faced planetexian wearing a large, ornate crown over a particularly transparent brain-sack. She sat on a huge green throne, surrounded by gleaming green statues of herself.

"Citizens of Planet X, it seems like only yesterday that I sent my armies to invade this fair globe, so that we could rebuild and remake it as the new Planet X. But now the time has come to invade once more! The votes have been counted and verified, and the four finalists have been chosen. So without further ado, the result! I love this bit. . ." said Empress Valoona as she hopped off her throne. She was blindfolded and handed a large drawing pin. She was pointed in the vague direction of a huge green map featuring four distinctive planets.

Hex, meanwhile, quickly realized that everyone had forgotten about him. Even the assisto-bots were too busy watching the holo-screen to pay him any attention. He got slowly to his feet, and caught sight of his reflection in one of the assisto-bot's well-polished chest panels. He was barely recognizable! He edged out of the ingestion zone as quietly as he could, being careful not to arouse suspicion or leave a trail of gloop for anyone to follow. He had just made it to the pupil purification pod when he heard the cry ring out across the loudspeakers.

"THE EMPRESS HAS CHOSEN! THE NEXT PLANET TO BE INVADED WILL BE . . . EARTH!"

A BRIEF HISTORY

Hex sneaked out of the pupil purification pod. He was making his way back to the ingestion zone when he was met by a sea of excited children coming towards him. He was carried along the corridor, through the hall and out to the landing zone. He had just started to wonder what all the fuss was about when Opo grabbed him by the arm.

"Hex! Where did you go?" she said. "You missed all the excitement!"

"I . . . er, toilet! I had to go to the relief zone. What's happening? Where's everyone going?" asked Hex.

"Home!" said Opo. "Didn't you hear? The Empress

picked a planet! We're on holiday for the rest of the day!"

"But. . ." began Hex, not quite believing he'd managed to escape disintegration.

"Oh, and don't worry, no one recognized you under all that gloop. Well, nearly no one," whispered Opo with a smile.

"I . . . I don't know what you mean," began Hex, as he followed Opo, Dooper and Steek on to their skybus.

"You OK, Hex? What happened to you back there?" asked Dooper, sliding into the seat next to Hex and squashing him against the window.

"I'll tell you later," said Hex, scraping dried gloop out of his gills. "Let's just say I *really* need to fix my tele-belt."

"You know what I heard?" said Steek, flicking Hex's hear lobe. "I heard that earthlings don't even have antennae!"

"My dad says they're blue!" said another boy. "Blue and scaly!"

Before long, everyone on the ship had joined in:

"They have no skin!"

"They smell like nudlork vomit!"

"They shoot fire out of their mouths!"

"They eat each other for fun!"

"They're ninety-six per cent pure evil!"

By the time Hex got home, he wasn't sure what to believe about earthlings. Everyone seemed to have their own idea about them. All he did know was that he wanted to be a space invader less than ever.

"Welcome home, Hex – and death to all earthlings!" cried T.K.

"Oh, so you heard," said Hex, dragging his feet through the front portal.

"It's all over the news-vids! Earth! I almost blew a circuit when I heard."

"So, how was your first day?" said Hex's mother as Hex took off his magna-boots. "Not *too* eventful, I hope."

"Great, just great," sighed Hex, unclipping his P.A.D. and dropping his massive tele-belt on the floor. "This boy on the skybus knew all about Dad, so now everyone thinks I'm bad luck."

"Hex, how many times do I have to tell you, there's no such thing as bad luck," said his mother. "The Hex Effect isn't real. As far as I'm concerned it was made up as a way of getting out of space invading."

"Oh yeah? Well, if there's no Hex Effect, then how do you explain my tele-belt exploding? Or my P.A.D. going crazy the second I turned it on? Or me ending up inside a giant gloop tube? If that's not bad luck then I don't know what is! I mean, I got sentenced to disintegration! On my first day!"

Hex's mother took a deep breath, and sighed a long sigh. "I'm sure there's a very simple explanation."

"Oh *really*? Great! That explains everything, then. Panic over. I'm just doomed, that's all, nothing to worry about! Maybe I can get sucked into a black hole too! At least I wouldn't have to be a space invader!" growled Hex, his antenna glowing green. After a moment, he sighed a long sigh and added, "Can I be excused? I need to try and fix this tele-belt."

"What about dinner?" asked his mother, a little taken aback.

"No thanks," said Hex, shuddering. "I'm all glooped out for today."

Hex made his way to his zone and laid the tele-belt out on his slumber pod. He was about to get to work repairing it when he remembered that Glitch was still in his pocket. He placed him next to the tele-belt and stared at them both.

"Well, I did *promise* to fix you," he said, setting the tele-belt aside. "And anyway, I'm pretty sure you're the only thing on this whole planet that has nothing to do with space invading."

Hex spent the next three hours putting Glitch back together. He reattached his head, popped out his dents and reconnected his coupling rods. Finally, stifling his yawns, Hex popped open the control panel on the back of Glitch's head and tweaked his primary control module. One by one, Glitch's arms whirled around, his head turned from side to side and he rolled back and forth, as if he was doing a particularly rubbish dance. It was almost bedtime by the time Hex flicked Glitch's ON switch.

"POP-klik-POP!" said Glitch. He spun his head around gleefully and started rolling around Hex's slumber pod.

"You're welcome!" said Hex. A moment later, his mother poked her head around the portal.

"I brought you a bowl of gloop," said his mother, coming into his zone. "You know what they say – you can't invade on an empty stomach. Did you manage to get your tele-belt fixed?"

"What? Oh yes, good as new!" said Hex, throwing a pillow over Glitch.

"I've ordered you a new one – it should arrive in a couple of days," said his mother, setting the gloop on his bedside table. "Can't have you at a disadvantage if you're going to become a first-rate space invader! Who knows? You might even get to invade Earth!"

"Great," said Hex, adding, "Mum . . . are earthlings *really* ninety-six per cent pure evil?"

"I heard ninety eight," said his mother, kissing him on the head. "Now go to sleep – it's another big day of training tomorrow." As his mother left, Hex lifted the pillow off Glitch.

"That was close. I don't think Mum would be too happy to see you around."

"POP-chik!" said Glitch, dashing nervously back under the pillow.

"Good idea, stay out of sight," laughed Hex. He climbed into his slumber pod, but his head was too full of thoughts of Planet Earth for him to sleep. He turned on his P.A.D. and said, "Tell me about Earth."

The P.A.D. pinged into life.

IT LOOKS LIKE YOU ARE TRYING TO INVADE PLANET EARTH. CAN I HELP?

"What? No!" began Hex, but the P.A.D. carried on all the same.

YOUR P.A.D. CAN HELP YOU DECIDE WHICH METHOD OF INVASION SUITS YOU BEST:
HYPERSAUCER ATTACK
LONG RANGE DISINTEGRATION RAY

MIND CONTROL SPORES

OR A METHOD OF YOUR CHOOSING. THERE ARE LOADS OF GREAT WAYS TO TAKE OVER THAT STINKING MUD BALL KNOWN AS EARTH! REDUCE IT TO RUBBLE OR DISGUISE YOURSELF AS AN EARTHLING AND TAKE OVER FROM THE INSIDE - YOU DECIDE!

"No, I mean, I want to *know* about Earth. What's it really like?" asked a frustrated Hex.

PING!

ALL ABOUT EARTH - A BRIEF HISTORY OF A STINKING MUD BALL.
THE BIRTH OF EARTH
BILLIONS OF YEARS AGO, TWO FAIRLY RUBBISH PLANETS CALLED ERR AND THH CRASHED TOGETHER TO MAKE ONE COMPLETELY USELESS PLANET KNOWN AS EARTH. COMPOSED OF EIGHTEEN THOUSAND DIFFERENT KINDS OF MUD, EARTH IS THE DIRTIEST, MUCKIEST, MUDDIEST WORLD IN EXISTENCE.

Earth sounded like the worst planet in the universe! Maybe it could do with being invaded – it didn't sound like it could get any worse. Hex skipped ahead to the next chapter.

LIFE ON EARTH
EARTH WAS THE ONLY PLANET IN ITS GALAXY TO CREATE LIFE, BUT IT WAS STILL THE WORST AT DOING IT. GIVEN THAT EARTH WAS MADE ENTIRELY OF MUD, SO ARE ITS HORRIBLY UNIMPRESSIVE LIFE FORMS. KNOWN AS EARTHLINGS, THESE CREATURES SPEND THEIR DAYS WANDERING AROUND IN MUD, WHILE TALKING ABOUT MUD AND EATING MUD (THAT IS, IF THEY ARE NOT EATING EACH OTHER).

A picture of two earthlings appeared on the screen. They were a sort of pinky-brown colour, with two arms and legs and a strange wiry clump of hair on top of their heads. They didn't even have antennae! Hex got nervous just looking at them. Then he noticed a flashing green button appear on screen, which read "Dare you learn more?" He pressed it without thinking.

WATCH OUT, EARTHLINGS ABOUT!
EARTHLINGS ARE A HIGHLY AGGRESSIVE RACE AND HATE EVERYTHING. THEY ARE CONSTANTLY ANGRY AND SPEND ALL DAY HITTING EACH OTHER WITH STICKS. WHEN THEY RUN OUT OF STICKS, THEY RUN EACH OTHER OVER IN WHEELED VEHICLES OR SHOUT UNTIL THEIR HEADS EXPLODE. EARTHLINGS HATE EVERYTHING IN THE UNIVERSE, AND HAVE TWICE DECLARED OPEN WAR ON PLANET X, EVEN THOUGH THEY DID NOT KNOW IT EXISTED.
EARTHLINGS: BETTER OFF DISINTEGRATED. GET THEM BEFORE THEY GET US!
DID THIS ANSWER YOUR QUESTION? YES/NO

Hex had no idea a planet could be so terrible! Why did

earthlings hate Planet X (and everything) so much? Was it because they were made of mud? He felt like he had more questions than before. He was about to ask his P.A.D. another question when, **PING-PING-PING-PING-PING-PING-PING-PING!**

"No!" said Hex, grabbing the P.A.D. and frantically pressing the green button. "Don't break again!"

GH25P97Y6235R8TYH5U; 0YΓW4TQ358
RECEIVING / DECODING . . . PLEASE WAIT. . .

It was the message from before! Or something very much like it. Hex closed his eyes and crossed his suckers, hoping that it would magically fix itself like before. Then, as if in answer to his prayers, the pinging stopped. He slowly opened one eye. On the P.A.D.'s screen were two words:

HELLO HEX.

Hex dropped the P.A.D. in shock! How did it know his name?

"T.K., are you messing with my P.A.D.?" he asked.

"Negative!" said T.K. "It is a violation of imperial directive 89,012.2 to interfere with the property of Her Majestic Green, the Empress Valoona XIII. Laws are there to be obeyed."

Hex picked up the P.A.D. and peeked nervously at the screen.

> ## HELLO HEX. . .
> ## ARE YOU OUT THERE?

Hex looked around, suddenly worried that he was being spied on! What if someone had worked out that he was the boy in the gloop? He would be disintegrated for sure! But then again, what if it was some kind of test, some way of proving how much of a space invader he was? After a moment he took a deep gill-breath and said, "Hello?"

There was another **PING!**

> ## CONTACT HAS BEEN MADE. PLEASE WAIT.

The screen went blank. Hex huddled nervously in the corner of his room, staring at the P.A.D., waiting for something to happen, but the P.A.D.'s screen stayed blank.

"What was that all about?" he said.

"Ka-chik-POP!" said Glitch.

Finally, Hex decided that it was probably just the Hex Effect messing everything up again. Maybe this was just how things were going to be from now on – *unpredictable*. Hex wondered how his dad had managed to live with the Hex Effect for so long. *Not that I'll ever get the chance to ask him*, thought Hex with a sigh. He turned off his P.A.D. and put it under his pillow. Then he patted Glitch goodnight and decided it was probably for the best if he forgot all about today. In fact, Hex decided to pretend it had never even happened.

EARTH-MANIA

The next morning, Hex woke up feeling altogether better about things. The problems of the previous day felt like a distant memory, and Hex decided to try to get excited about space invading. Plus Glitch was as good as new, even if his old tele-belt wasn't. Hex whizzed through the cleansing and clothing zones, and then tucked his little robot into his pocket and hopped on to the conveyor.

"Good morning, Hex," said Hex's mother, when Hex appeared in the ingestion zone. "Have you heard the news?"

"What news?" asked Hex. His mother just grinned and turned on the news-vid.

"*Three months?*" asked Hex in amazement. "But that's so soon!"

"When Planet X invades, it doesn't mess around!" yelled T.K.

"But we just got settled here," sighed Hex.

"You know what they say – a planet can't be destroyed in a day," said his mother. "These things take time. Best to start as soon as possible!"

"I suppose," said Hex, heading towards the ejection chute. He stared at the P.A.D. on his belt and looked back. "Mum? Could my P.A.D. know my name?"

"Your *name*? Of course not," laughed his mother. "You should know that's impossible. Why do you ask?"

"No reason," said Hex. A second later he was fired on to the waiting platform. He could already hear Dooper shouting "BOOM!" as the skybus pulled up.

"HEX!" shouted Dooper as Hex clambered aboard. "I saved you a seat! It's another big day for Team Dooper and Hex! BOOM!"

"Thanks Dooper," said Hex with a smile, squeezing on to the seat next to him. Dooper may have been a little strange, but it was nice to have a sort of friend. Especially since all Hex's previous friends had been home-made robots.

"So, did you get your tele-belt fixed?" asked Dooper.

"Uh, I'm working on it," said Hex, and then noticed Dooper was wearing a holo-badge, which read EARTH GOES BOOM! Hex looked around. Everyone was wearing holo-badges, with slogans like GOODBYE EARTH / HELLO PLANET X! and EARTHLINGS: DISINTEGRATE ON SIGHT! And it wasn't just badges – the children were weighed down with

Earth-themed gadgets, gizmos and accessories. From Countdown Clocks (Only 2 Months, 3 Weeks, 6 Days, 19 Hours and 22 Minutes Till Invasion!) to Earthling Detectors (Detects Earthlings From up to 50 Miles Away!), every aspect of the impending invasion was covered.

Where did they get all this stuff? It's only been one day! thought Hex. He suddenly had a funny feeling in his digestion sack, somewhere between jealousy and apprehension. He stared out of the window at the empress's shimmering green palace, and wondered if she ever had doubts about all this space invading.

"What have you got against invading, anyway?" said Steek, prodding Hex from across the aisle. He was wearing a holo-badge that had EARTH SUCKS MUD! written on it. "You're haven't even got a holo-badge! What's the matter? Do you *like* earthlings or something?"

"What? No! Of course not!" said Hex, defensively. "I just didn't know all this stuff was available."

"You know what I think? I think you wish you were an earthling!" bellowed Steek, loudly enough for everyone to hear. "Earthling! Earthling! Earth – ow!"

Something hit Steek in the head, bouncing off and landing in Hex's lap. He looked down. It was a holo-badge which read BAD LUCK, EARTHLINGS!

"Keep it," said Opo, shoving Steek back into his chair. "I've got loads."

"Thanks, I think. . ." said Hex, as the skybus landed outside the school.

"Aren't you sick of being saved by a girl, Hex-37?" said Steek, grumpily.

"Aren't you sick of being shown up by your sister?" replied Hex. Steek just huffed and pushed his way off the skybus, and Hex, Dooper and Opo all grinned in unison.

Before long, everyone had filed into the hall where Headmaster Sporg was waiting.

"Welcome to another day of space invader training! Now, as I'm sure you're all aware, Her Majestic Green, the Empress Valoona, has chosen the stinking mud ball Earth to become the new Planet X!" said Headmaster Sporg. "And with fewer than three months to go before the invasion, we will be speeding up your training here at Sporg's! I'm sure you will be crushed to hear that instead of four and a half years of boring theory tests, you will be jumping straight to the practical stuff – a crash course in space invading!"

"Yay!" screamed the children (except for Hex).

"What we cannot teach you properly, we will teach you quickly, so that you'll be invasion ready as soon as possible!" continued Sporg. "Who knows, you might even graduate in time to invade Earth! And remember – *if in doubt, disintegrate!*"

"If in doubt, disintegrate!" shouted the children.

"Yes, exactly, that's what I just said! Now, this morning you shall be learning how to fly a hypersaucer!" boomed Sporg.

"Yay!" cried the children again (except for Hex, of

course – and Dooper, who this time shouted "BOOM!").

"SILENCE!" yelled Sporg. "You will be teleported directly into your very own hypersaucer simulation holo-pod! These holo-pods look, feel and smell just like you are piloting a real hypersaucer, but do not fear – you are perfectly safe! Follow the instructions on your P.A.D. – they will give you all the information you need on how to complete the training session. Good luck; I expect you all to pass with full marks! Now set your belts to 'receive' and stand by to be teleported!"

Not again, thought Hex, looking down at his rusty old tele-belt. Memories of being trapped in a gloop tube came flooding back and made his suckers clammy with nerves. He didn't dare imagine what might happen this time. Then again, staying in the hall again with Headmaster Sporg wasn't an option. He'd definitely be disintegrated this time. Hex crossed his suckers and turned the dial on his belt. It rattled and buzzed, and then he felt the tingle of the transport beam. . .

HYPERSAUCER TRAINING

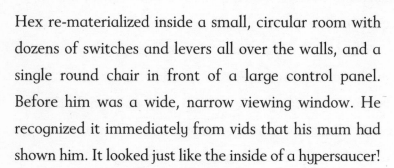

Hex re-materialized inside a small, circular room with dozens of switches and levers all over the walls, and a single round chair in front of a large control panel. Before him was a wide, narrow viewing window. He recognized it immediately from vids that his mum had shown him. It looked just like the inside of a hypersaucer!

"Glitch, it worked . . . it actually worked!" Hex said, putting Glitch on the hypersaucer control panel and patting his tele-belt with relief. He wandered around the holo-pod, inspecting every impressively realistic detail, and then made his way to the viewing window and peered out. It looked like a docking bay full of hundreds of hypersaucers!

"This is by far the most impressive holo-pod I've ever been in!" he said, hardly able to believe it wasn't real. Despite himself, Hex started to get excited about the idea of learning to fly. Space-invasion-related or not, it was still technology. Hex stared at the hypersaucer like it was a new toy, excited to know more about how it worked. He took his P.A.D. off his belt and stared at it. He hadn't turned it on since last night. He took a deep gill-breath.

"Now look, we got off to a bit of a bad start, you and me," Hex said to his P.A.D. "But I really think it'd be better for both of us if you just tell me what I need to know about flying a hypersaucer and we'll say no more about last night. How about it?"

Hex pressed the green button and the P.A.D. pinged into life and played its little jingle as normal. There was no sign of anything strange. Hex breathed a sigh of relief. He leaned in and said, "How do I fly a hypersaucer?"

IT LOOKS LIKE YOU ARE TRYING TO PILOT A
HYPERSAUCER. CAN I HELP?

"Yes! Yes, definitely!" cried Hex. He turned to Glitch
and said, "It's working!"

"Chik-POP!" said Glitch.

WELCOME TO HYPERSAUCER TRAINING. THIS
TUTORIAL WILL GUIDE YOU THROUGH
EVERYTHING YOU NEED TO KNOW ABOUT
PILOTING THE X9 HYPERSAUCER. THE HOLO-
POD WILL ALLOW YOU TO LEARN AND INVADE
IN A SAFE, SECURE ENVIRONMENT, WITHOUT
THE RISK OF ACCIDENTALLY DISINTEGRATING
SOMETHING YOU SHOULD NOT. PLEASE CHOOSE
A CHAPTER:
1) GETTING STARTED - TAKING OFF AND
   LANDING YOUR HYPERSAUCER
2) FINDING YOUR (DEEP) SPACE - HOW TO
   BREAK ORBIT
3) FASTER! FASTER! - MAKING THE HOP TO
   HYPERSPACE
4) AAAH! WATCH OUT FOR THAT WORMHOLE!
   THINGS TO LOOK OUT FOR IN SPACE

5) PUTTING THE GREAT IN DISINTEGRATE! — DEATH RAYS AND HOW TO FIRE THEM

6) WHAT GOES UP, MUST COME DOWN — YOUR HYPERSAUCER IS ABOUT TO CRASH, WHAT NEXT?

It was a baffling array of choices. Hex pressed 1 and hoped for the best.

GOOD CHOICE! PLEASE TREAT THIS SIMULATION AS IF YOU WERE PILOTING A REAL HYPERSAUCER. FIRST, PRESS THE GREEN START BUTTON.

Hex followed the instructions to the letter. He powered up the hypersaucer, de-clamped it from its moorings and then guided it as carefully as he could out of the docking bay.

GROOOORNCH! KRU-URNK!

"PROXIMITY ALERT! REVERSE!" said the hypersaucer's on-board computer as Hex bumped into a nearby ship!

"Sorry! Sorry!" said Hex. He checked his P.A.D. for further instructions.

CONGRATULATIONS! YOU ARE ON THE MOVE. NOW PRESS THE GO FASTER PEDAL, AND USE THE BIG, OBVIOUS LEVER TO MOVE AROUND. PUSH UP TO GO DOWN AND PULL DOWN TO GO UP! AND TRY NOT TO STALL!

Hex **CLANG!**ed and **GROORNK!**ed his way through the holo-hangar, crashing into a couple of holo-hypersaucers as he made his way out of the docking bay.

I'll probably get marked down for that, he thought. But then again, getting out of the hangar was surely the hardest part – it was all zooming through the skies and blowing stuff up from now on! For the first time in his life, Hex started to get excited about space invading. He swept out of the docking bay, and was confronted with something rather odd. Instead of a holographic Earth (which he rather expected to see) Hex was confronted with a holographic Planet X! It was a perfect recreation of New X City, down to the last detail, as real as the city he'd seen from the skybus only moments before. Hex leaned forward to get a better look, and stood on the GO FASTER pedal.

VWOOOOOOOOOOM!

Hex was thrown backwards as the hypersaucer rocketed into the sky!

"AAAH! Stop – wait, no one's flying! Glitch, hang on to something!" cried Hex. He scrambled back to his chair as the hypersaucer pranged the side of a conveyor bridge and sent it crashing to the ground.

"IMPACT ALERT!" said the computer in an urgent tone.

"Hope that doesn't affect my score!" said Hex, grabbing the big, obvious lever and pulling on it with both suckers. The hypersaucer stopped in mid-air. Hex stared up at the two suns of Planet X and breathed a sigh of relief. For a moment, everything was still – but only for a moment.

"ALERT! ALERT! PULL UP! IMPACT IN 5.2 SECONDS!" said the computer as the hypersaucer

rolled in the air and nose-dived back towards the ground!

"Th-this is re-really re-realist-tic!" said Hex, trying to keep control of the shuddering hypersaucer! He yanked the lever with all his might just as he was about to crash and the hypersaucer swooped upwards and whirled in the air, knocking into a transport ship and sending it into another ship, then another, like a game of exploding dominos!

"I th-think I'm getting the ha-hang of it. . .!" stammered Hex. In fact, once he'd stopped bouncing off holo-buildings and making ships crash into each other, he started to feel like a real pilot, and after a while he couldn't help but enjoy himself. He hit the GO FASTER pedal again and he was away! He zoomed through the skies, spiralling and weaving between buildings as if he were on a giant obstacle course. It was as though he'd been flying all his life! After a few minutes, he spotted a familiar sight out of the corner of the viewing portal.

"Glitch, look, it's Sporg's!" said Hex, holding Glitch up against the window. They were hovering over a perfect holo-version of Hex's school! There was even a large holo-crowd of planetexian children gathered outside, staring up at the hypersaucer or running about in panic. Everyone was down there – Dooper, Opo, even Steek, wearing his ᕮᗩᖇᎢᕼ ᔕᑌᑕᛕᔕ ᗰᑌᗪ! badge! Hex had never known a holo-pod to be so realistic! It seemed almost *impossible*.

Suddenly, Hex's jaw dropped open. He looked at his tele-belt and remembered what Opo had said to him: "*. . .you could re-materialize anywhere on Planet X!*"

Hex peered down at the much-too-realistic-to-be-holographic crowds of screaming children, then at the city, which smoked and smouldered in his path. As reality dawned, all the green drained out of Hex's face.

"Oh, no . . . this isn't a holo-pod at all," he said. "I teleported into an *actual* hypersaucer!"

The Hex Effect had struck again!

"Attention, enemy of PLANET X!" came a cry. "This is the PLANET X police! Surrender immediately so that we can disintegrate you . . . or be disintegrated! You have thirty seconds to comply!"

Two police skycars appeared in Hex's viewing portal . . . and then another three! He was completely surrounded!

"Wait! It's not my fault! I didn't know it was real!" cried Hex.

"Surrender! You have twenty seconds to comply!"

"I surrender! I surrender!" Hex screamed, pounding against the viewing window, but no one could see him. He grabbed his P.A.D. in desperation.

"P.A.D., help! I'm surrounded by police ships and they're going to disintegrate me!" he said. "What do I do?"

> IT SOUNDS LIKE YOU ARE UNDER ATTACK.
> CAN I-

"Yes! You can help!" shouted Hex.

> YOU ARE BEING ATTACKED BY ENEMY FORCES.
> DO NOT PANIC. THE X9 HYPERSAUCER IS
> EQUIPPED WITH AN IMPENETRABLE FORCE

FIELD, STEALTH MODE CAPABILITY, AS WELL
AS AN IMPRESSIVE ARRAY OF WEAPONRY.
FIRST, LOCATE YOUR FORCE-FIELD
ACTIVATION SWITCH, WHICH CAN BE
FOUND. . .

Suddenly, the P.A.D.'s screen went dead.

"Found where? Found WHERE?!?" screamed Hex.

RECEIVING / DECODING. . . PLEASE WAIT. . .

"No! Don't make me wait!" yelled Hex.

"You now have ten seconds to comply!" said the police
skycar.

PING!

"Ping? Ping *what*?!?" screamed Hex, shaking the
P.A.D. Then:

HELLO AGAIN, HEX.
IT'S NICE TO FINALLY MAKE CONTACT.

"No! Not *now*! Who are you? Leave me alone!" cried Hex.

"Five seconds!" said the police skycar.

"AAAH!" screamed Hex, pressing any button and pulling any lever that he could find! A cup holder appeared from the control panel and a disco ball dropped from the ceiling, but nothing that could save him from being blown to bits! By now, Glitch was zooming up and down the control panel, from button to button, desperate to find one that could help them.

"Ch-chick-POP! POP!" cried the little robot in panic.

"I know, I know, but which button? How about this one?" Hex said, pointing to a big green one.

"POP?" said Glitch with a shrug.

Hex clenched a sucker and punched the button!

ZWAAAAAAAAAAAAARK!

A death ray fired out from the hypersaucer! It blasted a nearby teleportation tower, disintegrating it in an explosion of light!

"Oops. . ." muttered Hex. Glitch just shook his head.

"He's fighting back! Blast him!" cried the police ship,

and a volley of death rays beamed out from each skycar! Hex's hypersaucer shook with the impact as it was bombarded from all sides!

BOOM! K-KROOM!

"ALERT! HULL BREACH! DESTRUCTION IMMINENT!" cried the hypersaucer's on-board computer.

"Glitch, hang on!" screamed Hex, grabbing hold of his robot as the control panel exploded in a shower of sparks! He popped open the control panel on his tele-belt.

Oh why didn't I fix the belt? thought Hex, and whacked the tele-belt as hard as he could! Suddenly, the tele-belt began to fizzle and spark. Then (1.2 seconds later) the hypersaucer exploded into one million and sixty-two pieces.

BOOOOOOOOOOOOOOOOOOOM!!

DROP AND COWER

"Where . . . whuh . . . how?" said Hex, re-materializing in the school hall. His tele-belt had worked! It had transported him out of the hypersaucer a second before it exploded! Hex slumped to the floor in relief.

"I'm OK . . . I'm alive!" he said, staring at his open suckers in disbelief. "That was close. Really, *really* – wait a minute, where's Glitch?"

"Clik-bzzt!" came the tiny, muffled reply. Hex leapt to his feet. He'd sat on Glitch! Hex picked up the flattened robot and tried to put Glitch's eye back into his head.

"Not again! Glitch, say something! Give me a sign! A click, a pop, anything!" said Hex, but Glitch just sparked a bit as his head came loose. "Oh, Glitch, I'm sorry. You'll be OK, I'll fix you, I promise."

Hex was just tucking Glitch into his pocket when he heard a commotion coming from outside the school. The hypersaucer had exploded – maybe debris from the explosion had fallen on top of someone! Hex hurried cautiously out of the hall to see pupils, teachers and assisto-bots alike running around in panic.

"We've been invaded!" screamed one child.

"The earthlings are attacking!" yelled another.

"They're invading us before we can invade them!" shrieked a third. Hex tried to make his way back into the school, but was shoved and jostled by panicking pupils until a pair of large green suckers dragged him out of the crowd.

"Hex! You're OK!" It was Dooper. He dragged Hex to his feet and hugged him so hard Hex thought his telepathy nodes might burst. "I thought you'd been disintegrated by earthlings!" said Dooper.

"Earthlings? What earthlings?" asked Hex. "Why is everyone talking about earthlings?"

"Earthlings stole a hypersaucer and tried to destroy the city!" cried Opo, scrambling out of the crowd. "They're invading us before we get to invade them!"

"Wait, everyone thinks *earthlings* were in that hypersaucer?" said Hex, and then suddenly saw the bright side – if everyone was blaming the earthlings for the hypersaucer "attack", they weren't blaming him! He decided the best thing to do was join in.

"Yeah, of *course* it was earthlings! Why, they're probably planning their next attack right now!" said Hex, loudly.

Before long almost everyone was screaming and running about in terror. Pupils climbed over each other to get away, even though no one knew where they were going. Steek was the loudest, screaming, "Someone protect me! I'm going to be the greatest space invader ever! You need me alive and undisintegrated!" In fact, it wasn't until more police skycars arrived to move everyone inside that anyone did what they were told.

"Everyone, move inside in a calm, orderly fashion!" came the cry from the police skycars. "By order of the PLANET X police department! Stay calm; panicking and hysterical waving of suckers in panic is prohibited!"

Once the pupils had calmed down and regrouped, they teleported back to their learning pods. Even Hex, whose tele-belt *finally* seemed to be behaving itself. Miss Voob stood at the front of the class, nervously wringing her suckers. No one seemed to know what to do now that Planet X had apparently been invaded. It had never happened before! They were the ones who did the invading!

Finally, Miss Voob had an idea. She unclipped her P.A.D. and plugged it into the holo-screen generator. A large holo-screen appeared in the air. She leaned into the P.A.D. and asked, tensely, "What do we do if *we're* invaded?"

PING!

> IT LOOKS LIKE YOUR PLANET IS BEING
> INVADED BY A HOSTILE ALIEN RACE. CAN I
> HELP?

"YES!" shouted the whole class.

> AN INVASION MAY PROVE AN UNWELCOME
> DISTRACTION IN THE LIFE OF A SPACE
> INVADER. KNOWING HOW TO REACT IN THE
> EVENT OF SUCH AN ATTACK IS VITAL.
> FORTUNATELY, THE PLANETEXIAN DEFENCE
> COUNCIL OF PLANETARY DEFENCE HAS
> DEVELOPED A FOOLPROOF METHOD OF
> PROTECTING YOURSELF AGAINST ANY KIND
> OF INVASION: DROP AND COWER!

"Yay! Drop and Cower!" shouted Dooper, adding, "What's Drop and Cower?"

The holo-screen showed a picture of a happy planetexian hiding underneath a desk.

> LITTLE VEEP, OUR HAPPY PLANETEXIAN,
> KNOWS THAT WHEN INVASION COMES, THE

ONLY WAY TO BE SAFE IS TO DROP AND
COWER! FIRST, DROP TO THE FLOOR, AND
THEN FIND COVER UNDERNEATH A TABLE OR
CHAIR. THEN, COWER THERE, COVERING YOUR
HEAD WITH YOUR
SUCKERS. THAT
WAY, WHEN THE
INVADERS COME,
YOU WILL BE SAFE.

REMEMBER, DROP
AND COWER!

"That's the stupidest thing I've ever heard," said Hex.

"Drop and Cower! Drop and Cower!" yelled Dooper,
excitedly.

For the rest of the morning, Roswell class practised
Drop and Cower, much to Hex's disbelief – they even
missed lunch!

"Hey! Hey, Hex!" said Dooper, as Hex tried to get
comfortable under his desk. "Them earthlings will
never get us now! They can invase all they like, we'll
just Drop and Cower! Then when they've run out of
death rays, BOOM! We invase them good! Team

Dooper and Hex does it again! BOOM!"

Hex shook his head. For a second he considered telling Miss Voob the truth, just so he wouldn't have to hide under this desk all day, but then he remembered the message from his P.A.D. He took it off his tele-belt and looked at it.

I'M STILL HERE.

Hex almost dropped his P.A.D. in shock. It was still on! "Leave me alone!" he whispered. "You're messing up my P.A.D.! And I really don't need anything else to mess up!"

There was a pause.

THINGS NOT GOING TOO WELL?

"Never mind how things are going! There's no way a P.A.D. can know your name! What's going on?"

YOUR P.A.D. DOESN'T KNOW YOUR NAME, BUT I DO.

"What? You mean, you're a *someone*? I mean, you're real?" whispered Hex, more anxious than ever.

OF COURSE! I WOULD HAVE CONTACTED YOU SOONER, BUT I COULDN'T RISK IT. IF ANYONE FOUND OUT YOU WERE COMMUNICATING WITH THE OUTSIDE UNIVERSE, YOU COULD BE DISTINTEGRATED!

"The outside *universe*? I don't understand!" whispered Hex. "Who are you? What do you want?"

I WANT TO LET YOU KNOW THERE'S MORE TO LIFE THAN SPACE INVADING.

"What do you mean?" said Hex, remembering that this could all be part of some secret test, some part of his invader training. "I . . . I *like* space invading! Everyone does!"

> **DO YOU THINK YOU'RE THE ONLY PLANETEXIAN WHO DOESN'T WANT TO BE A SPACE INVADER? EVEN YOU'RE NOT THAT UNLUCKY.**

"How . . . how do you know about my luck?" whispered Hex.

There was a pause.

> **BAD LUCK RUNS IN THE FAMILY.**

Hex gasped, his eyes wide.

"D-Dad?"

LOST (DAD) IN SPACE

TIME UNTIL INVASION - 92 DAYS, 4 HOURS, 33 MINUTES

"ATTENTION CITIZENS OF PLANET X! HER MAJESTIC GREEN, THE EMPRESS VALOONA XIII, IS ABOUT TO ADDRESS HER SUBJECTS!" The announcement boomed out all across the school.

No! Not now! thought Hex.

"Stop Dropping and Cowering children, and pay attention!" said Miss Voob, as another holo-screen materialized in the middle of the learning pod.

"Dad? Is that really you?" Hex whispered into his P.A.D. as he crouched under his desk. "Where are you? How did you find me? Where have you been all this—"

"That means you too, Hex," commanded Miss Voob. "The empress demands your full and undivided attention! If I see you playing with that P.A.D., I shall confiscate it, simple as that." Losing his P.A.D. now was the last thing Hex needed, so he hurriedly tucked it into his belt. A moment later, the empress's fat face appeared on the holo-screen.

"Citizens of Planet X, it is with a heavy heart and damp gills that I bring you this news. Planet X is being invaded! Earlier today, New X City was attacked by a stolen hypersaucer, piloted by an earthling spy!" said the empress.

Now even the empress thinks it's an earthling invasion! thought Hex, a bead of sweat running down his brain-sack. Now more than ever, he knew that telling the truth was completely out of the question.

"The earthling was disintegrated, but the threat remains!" continued the empress. "Who knows how many earthlings are in hiding on Planet X, waiting to strike? They could be anywhere! Hiding in our places of work, our schools, even our homes! Well, obviously not my home – the palace is much too well protected. But the rest of you could be invaded at any moment!"

"AAAH! Drop and Cower! Drop and Cower!" cried Steek.

"Well, I say, bring 'em on!" continued the empress. "We'll show these earthlings who they're messing with! And to prove I mean business, I am bringing forward the invasion of Earth! My space invader army will now launch *tomorrow*, at twenty o'clock exactly! Let's see how much fight they have in them after we've reduced their planet to rubble! Ha!"

A cheer went up from the class. Hex took advantage of the distraction to take his P.A.D. off his belt.

"Dad?" he whispered.

> **THERE YOU ARE!**
> **THOUGHT I'D LOST YOU FOR A MINUTE.**

"The Empress is giving a speech about the next invasion – it's happening tomorrow!" said Hex.

> **I PITY THE POOR PLANET SHE'S PICKED ON THIS TIME. I'M**
> **SURE IF THE EMPRESS SPENT ANY TIME ON ANOTHER**
> **WORLD SHE'D LEARN TO LOVE IT. I KNOW I HAVE.**

"You're on another world?" whispered Hex in disbelief. "How? What happened to you in space?"

MY HYPERSAUCER GOT SUCKED INTO A BLACK HOLE – JUST MY LUCK! FINALLY I STRAYED UPON ANOTHER PLANET, AND MANAGED TO CRASH-LAND. I'VE BEEN HERE EVER SINCE!

"Here where?" whispered Hex. "Where are you?"

IT'S A STRANGE LITTLE WORLD ON THE FAR REACHES OF THE NEXT GALAXY. I'M ON A PLANET CALLED—

"Hex!" screeched Miss Voob, snatching the P.A.D. from Hex's suckers. "What did I tell you about playing with your P.A.D. when the empress is talking?"

"Sorry! I didn't mean to! I was just—" began Hex, panicking.

"Rules are rules, Hex. I don't think you want to end up in the disintegration pod, now do you?" said Miss Voob, clipping Hex's P.A.D. on to her belt. "You can have it back at the end of the day. Now everyone teleport down to training zone 42 – it's time for your ray-gun training."

"Death rays! Finally! BOOM!" cried Dooper.

Hex watched as the other pupils de-materialized, until he was left alone with Miss Voob.

"Um, I don't suppose. . .?" he began, pointing at his P.A.D. Miss Voob just tapped it, and then activated her tele-belt.

"You'll get it back when I feel confident you will use it properly," she said, as she began to teleport. "What's so important it can't wait until then?"

RAY-GUN TRAINING

Hex thought about begging Miss Voob to give him his P.A.D. back, but in the end he decided he would simply have to wait until she had a change of circulation organ. Hex set his tele-belt to receive, and (much to his relief) re-materialized in training zone 42. Miss Voob was already handing out ray-guns.

"There are two very important things to remember about your ray-gun," said Miss Voob. "Which is the safe end, and which is the dangerous end. Memorize these ends quickly, or else your life as a space invader will be very short-lived."

Hex gulped as Miss Voob handed him a silver, oval-shaped ray-gun. After the morning he'd had, the last thing he wanted to do was shoot things.

"Your ray-guns have three settings: disintegrate, stun and mutate," said Miss Voob, pointing to a small dial on the side of the ray-gun. "Do not get these settings confused. The last thing you want to do is mutate an angry earthling into a winged Zorlock – it will only make your job more difficult. As Headmaster Sporg says – if in doubt, disintegrate!"

"If in doubt, disintegrate!" repeated the children.

"That said, we shall begin with the stun setting, so please set your dials and we shall begin. Can I have a volunteer?"

Hex reluctantly turned the dial on his ray-gun, but it ended up getting stuck on mutate. No matter how hard he tried, he couldn't move it.

"Stupid Hex Effect . . . come on!" he grumbled, putting his sucker in the air. "Uh, Miss Voob, I don't think my ray-gun is—"

"We have a volunteer! Thank you, Hex-37."

"What? No, I wasn't volunteering, I. . ." began Hex, but Miss Voob ignored him.

"Now then, Hex has kindly volunteered to be the first to be shot with the stun ray," said Miss Voob, ushering Hex to the other end of the training zone.

"I did what?!" said Hex, frantically. "No, wait, I was just trying to tell you that—"

"I'll shoot him, Miss Voob!" cried Steek. "Can I? Can I, please?"

"How nice to see such a keen student," said Miss Voob. "Very well, Steek – take aim."

"But . . . I don't want to be shot!" protested Hex, rather surprised that he had to spell it out.

"Oh, do calm down, Hex. *Everyone* gets to shoot someone in ray-gun training – it's just a matter of who goes first. Now hold still, this won't hurt a bit. Well, obviously it'll hurt a *bit* – but it shouldn't do any lasting damage, with any luck. . ."

"Hey Hex. . . Boom," sneered Steek, and fired!

ZWAAARK!

The stun ray shot out of Steek's ray-gun! The ray

zoomed past Hex's head and bounced off the wall.

"Hey, no fair – he's moving!" said Steek and fired again, but the stun ray missed again, whizzing over the top of Hex's antenna.

"Don't worry, Hex, Steek's always been a terrible shot!" chuckled Opo. "He couldn't hit a Giant Brompuss from twenty paces!"

"Shut up, Opo! I'm a great shot!" cried Steek, firing three times in a row!

ZWAAARK! ZWAARK! ZWAARK!

"Knock it off!" yelled Hex, as the stun rays zoomed past him. Then, as he tried to cover his face with his suckers, he dropped his ray-gun! Hex watched the gun fall to the ground as if in slow motion, until, finally it bounced on the ground . . . and fired!

ZWAAAARK!

The ray hit Hex in the chest, throwing him against the wall!

"Ha! He shot himself!" laughed Steek. "Didn't I say the Hex Effect was real? He's got the worst luck ever!"

"Hex! Are you OK?" cried Dooper.

"I don't . . . feel so good," said Hex, looking down at his suckers. Suddenly, instead of the regular two – there were four! Hex was mutating!

"Aah! Help!" he shouted, as he sprouted thick green fur all over his body! Then his legs turned into long tentacles and wings sprouted out of his back!

"He's turned into a monster! No, wait – an earthling! Shoot him!" said Steek. The panicking pupils took aim, and fired on Hex! Hex screamed and flapped his wings, which carried him into the air.

"Help! I'm flying without the aid of an anti-gravity generator!" cried Hex.

"I'll help – and this time I won't miss," said Steek, switching his ray-gun setting to disintegrate.

"Steek, don't you dare!" said Opo, firing her ray-gun at him. It blasted out with uncanny accuracy and hit him in the head. Steek fell, stunned, to the floor! In the turmoil, everyone started firing their ray-guns – at Hex, at each other, even at Miss Voob!

"All right, that's enough of that! Stop firing! I said, stop—"

ZWAAARK!

Miss Voob was shot in the bottom from a stray beam! As she slumped, limply, to the floor, Headmaster Sporg materialized in the middle of the room. He surveyed the chaos in horror. "Will someone tell me exactly what on Planet X is going on?"

THE PROBLEM WITH PLANET EARTH

> **TIME UNTIL INVASION - 22 HOURS, 3 MINUTES**

As it was almost impossible to work out who was to blame for the disastrous ray-gun lesson, Headmaster Sporg decided to spare everyone from disintegration. That, and the fact that Empress Valoona needed all the space invaders she could get in the fight against the earthlings.

Everyone in the class had a visit to the medical zone for Stun Therapy, except for Hex, who was sent straight to the de-mutation zone. One de-mutation pill later, he was feeling very much himself. In fact, by the time he left school, he had lost his wings, hair, and even his extra limbs. He looked entirely planetexian.

"Hex!" said Hex's mum as Hex made his way to the landing zone with Dooper.

"Mum! What are you doing here?" asked Hex, double-checking he didn't still have a tail.

"I was at the hypersaucer hangar, inspecting the empress's new fleet, when one of the hypersaucers was stolen by the earthlings! I've been here at the crash site most of the afternoon, helping with enquiries. The whole planet is on high alert!" said his mum. "Did you see anything? Are you all right?"

In that moment, despite everything, Hex decided not to tell his mum about the hypersaucer, or even about his dad. He wanted to trust her, but he knew, deep down, she put space invading before anything else. If she found out about everything, disintegration would be the least of Hex's worries.

"I . . . uh, I'm fine," he said, nervously. "To be honest, I didn't even *see* the hypersaucer attack. I guess . . . I guess I was just too busy with my training."

"Well it's good to see you finally taking an interest," said Hex's mum. "I told you you'd enjoy space invading if you gave it a go."

"Hey, Hex! Wait!" said Opo, running up to Hex just as he was about to leave. "Glad to see you're yourself again."

"Thanks. Nice shooting, back there," replied Hex.

"No problem – I've been wanting to shoot Steek for ages!" She giggled. She turned to go, but then stopped. She took something out of her pocket and pressed it into Hex's sucker. "I found this amongst the bits of the crashed hypersaucer. It's a bit disintegrated around the edges, but. . ."

Hex looked down. It was his BAD LUCK, EARTHLINGS! holo-badge – half-disintegrated and still smouldering. Hex stared at it in horror. It must have fallen off in the hypersaucer! He'd been found out!

"Your secret's safe with me," Opo whispered. Then, with a wink, she hopped on the skybus.

"Who was that?" asked Hex's mum. "A friend of yours?"

"I guess so. . ." said Hex, scratching his head in bewilderment.

"HEX-37!" came a cry. Hex recognized Miss Voob's voice immediately. He froze, sure that he was about to be sentenced to disintegration or "volunteered" to be shot at again. He turned nervously to see Miss Voob striding towards him.

"Here, I thought you might like this back," she said, pressing his P.A.D. into his suckers. "I'm *sure* you'll use it properly from now on, won't you?"

"Yes, Miss," replied Hex, sheepishly.

"Well, I'm glad to see you're so popular, Hex – with pupils and teachers alike!"

"Heh . . . yeah, I'm a real hit," said Hex, clipping his P.A.D. to his belt. He didn't dare turn it on when his mother was around.

"Well, I'm proud of you, Hex," said his mum as she led him to her skycar. "It's good to see you applying yourself and not messing around with robots. You'll be a great space invader yet, I'm sure of it."

*

At home, Hex polished off two surprisingly tasty bowls of gloop, and then made his way to his zone. He quickly turned on his P.A.D. to see if his dad was still online, but the screen was blank. He took off his tele-belt and laid it on his slumber pod, and then remembered Glitch was still in his pocket. He stared at them both.

"Well, it is my fault you're in this state," he said to Glitch. He set his tele-belt aside again and popped open Glitch's control panel. By the time he'd triple-checked Glitch's primary control module, the suns had set over Planet X, and it was too late to fix the tele-belt.

"POP-chik!" said Glitch, as Hex turned him on.

"Sorry, Glitch, it's too late to play," sighed Hex. "Who knows what'll be in store for me at school tomorrow . . . I'd better get some—"

PING!

"Glitch, I said it's – wait . . . was that you?" whispered Hex.

"Klik-POP?" replied Glitch.

PING! PING! PING! PING! PING!

"It's the P.A.D.!" said Hex, grabbing the P.A.D. off his tele-belt. "Dad! Dad, is that you?"

HEX, WHAT HAPPENED ?

"I had a little P.A.D. trouble," said Hex. "And tele-belt trouble and hypersaucer trouble, and ray-gun trouble. . ."

SOUNDS LIKE THE HEX EFFECT . . . THAT THING HAS BEEN FOLLOWING US AROUND FOR YEARS. WE'RE JUST NOT CUT OUT FOR SPACE INVADING.

"Mum says there's no such thing as the Hex Effect," said Hex. "She said you just didn't want to be a space invader."

AND WHAT DO YOU BELIEVE?

"I . . . I don't know. I'm usually so good with technology, but when it comes to space invading, nothing works. It doesn't make sense. The Hex Effect must be real. Steek's right . . . we're bad luck.

JUST BECAUSE THE HEX EFFECT IS REAL, THAT DOESN'T MEAN IT'S BAD.

"What do you mean?" asked Hex.

YOU'LL SEE. IT MIGHT SEEM LIKE BAD LUCK RIGHT NOW, BUT IT ALL DEPENDS ON HOW YOU LOOK AT IT. YOU NEED TO TRUST THE HEX EFFECT, NOT FEAR IT.

"I don't understand," said Hex.

THE FACT IS, HEX, I HATED SPACE INVADING. I HATED EVERYTHING TO DO WITH IT. I REMEMBER ONE DAY I WISHED THAT I COULD BE ANYTHING ELSE . . . . THAT I COULD DO ANYTHING ELSE, AS LONG AS IT WASN'T SPACE INVADING. THE NEXT MINUTE, I WAS SUCKED INTO A BLACK

> HOLE, AND FOUND MYSELF HERE, ON THIS DISTANT PLANET . . . THIS WONDERFUL PLANET, WHERE THERE IS NO SUCH THING AS SPACE INVADING.

"No space invading?" said Hex, his eyes glazing over at the thought of it. "That sounds like the best planet ever!"

> WELL, I DON'T KNOW ABOUT THAT, BUT IT'S BETTER THAN PLANET X! THAT'S WHY I'VE BEEN TRYING TO CONTACT YOU – I WANT YOU TO JOIN ME.

"What? Me? How?" cried Hex.

> IT'S NOT GOING TO BE EASY – BUT IT'LL BE WORTH IT IN THE END. I'M SURE YOU'LL LOVE IT HERE ON EARTH.

Hex froze. He read the words again and again, just to be sure.

"Did . . . did you say Earth?" he said, quietly.

"PLANET X IS INVADING EARTH! TOMORROW! They're going to blow Earth to bits and turn it into the next Planet X!"

There was a pause.

NOW, THAT IS BAD LUCK.

HOLO-SUIT TRAINING

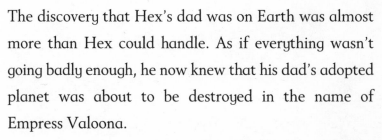

> TIME UNTIL INVASION - 4 HOURS 13 MINUTES

The discovery that Hex's dad was on Earth was almost more than Hex could handle. As if everything wasn't going badly enough, he now knew that his dad's adopted planet was about to be destroyed in the name of Empress Valoona.

Hex had spent the entire night talking to his father on his P.A.D., devising some way of saving Earth from destruction. They didn't come up with anything – Hex's father just kept telling him to "trust in the Hex Effect". The only thing they had both agreed on was that it was probably better not to tell Hex's mum. Neither of them wanted her to be put in danger – and if they were honest, neither of them were really sure where her loyalties lay.

When morning came, Hex just tucked Glitch into his pocket, ate his gloop quietly and made his way to the waiting platform without a word.

"Hey Hex! Come and sit with me! I've made up an invasion song to celebrate invasing day!" cried Dooper. The song (called "Earth Goes BOOM!") was tuneless but surprisingly entertaining and before long the entire skybus was singing along. Hex, however, sat in silence, wondering how to stop Earth from being invaded.

Still, nothing came to mind. How could Hex save his dad?

"Well, I hope you've all recovered from the excitement of yesterday," said Miss Voob as Roswell class materialized into the learning pod. "I for one have a terrible stun-ray headache ... so the first pupil to misbehave gets disintegrated. Now, listen carefully, Roswell class!" she said. "Today you will learn that *disguise* is a crucial weapon in the space invader's arsenal. You will learn how to master the holo-suit, and disguise yourself as a mud-sucking earthling! Set your tele-belts to receive – we're beaming down to training zone 78. And let's have no more *problems*, please. Good luck!"

"We're gonna dress up like earthlings!" said Dooper, nudging Hex in the shoulder. "They'll never see us coming! Team Dooper and Hex, in disguise! And before you know it . . . BOOM!"

Hex wasn't listening. He was too busy worrying about his dad to think about anything else. He turned the dial on his tele-belt as the teleportation beam bathed them in blue light.

"We'll be the heroes of Planet X!" continued Dooper. Hex opened his eyes. It worked! He'd been teleported to training zone 78 with the rest of Roswell class. Miss Voob was standing at the front of the class on a large crate, and holding what looked like a shimmering green jumpsuit.

"This is a holo-suit. There is one for each of you. Collect it, and then follow the instructions on your

P.A.D.," said Miss Voob, and then stared at Hex. "And don't make me regret giving you yours back, Hex-37."

"Um . . . P.A.D., how do I look like an earthling?" he asked quickly, desperate not to have his P.A.D. confiscated again.

IT LOOKS LIKE YOU ARE TRYING TO DISGUISE YOURSELF AS AN EARTHLING. CAN I HELP?

"Yeah, I guess," replied Hex.

YOUR HOLO-SUIT HAS BEEN TAILORED TO GENERATE A HOLOGRAPHIC IMAGE OF AN EARTHLING OVER THE WEARER. YOU WILL LEARN TO LOOK AND ACT LIKE AN EARTHLING, SO THAT YOU CAN BLEND IN WITH THEM, AND GET CLOSE ENOUGH TO DISINTEGRATE THEM WITHOUT HAVING TO WORRY ABOUT BEING DISCOVERED. PLEASE CHOOSE A CHAPTER:
1) GETTING THE LOOK - PUTTING ON YOUR HOLO-SUIT
2) FINGERS, NOT SUCKERS - UNDERSTANDING EARTHLING ANATOMY

Hex pressed 1, hoping that his dad would get in touch at any moment with a brilliant idea . . . but instead:

FIRST, GET INTO YOUR HOLO-SUIT. YOUR PRE-PROGRAMMED EARTHLING DISGUISE WILL ACTIVATE AS SOON AS YOU FASTEN THE ZIP.

Hex reluctantly pulled the holo-suit over his head. As the rest of Roswell class did the same, Hex saw them transform into earthlings before his eyes! They looked just like the picture he'd seen on his P.A.D. They were various shades of pink or brown, with a clump of wiry hair on their heads and dull, un-silvery clothing. They looked perfectly earthling-like!

NOW YOU LOOK LIKE AN EARTHLING IT IS
TIME TO START ACTING LIKE ONE. AS
EARTHLINGS HATE EVERYTHING, THEY ARE
ANGRY WITH EVERYTHING. START BY
GRUNTING, GROWLING AND EVEN HISSING
WHENEVER YOU COME IN CONTACT WITH
ANOTHER CREATURE. IF YOU CAN FIND A
STICK OR BLUNT INSTRUMENT, FEEL FREE TO
BASH THINGS WITH IT.

"Uh oh. . ." mumbled Hex. He spent the rest of the morning trying to avoid being hit by a vengeful Steek, with limited success. As he was much too distracted to fight back, Steek took full advantage of his "bashing rights", pummelling Hex with whatever he could get his hands on, and shouting things like, "I'm beating you earthling-style!" and "Eat my muddy fury!"

By the time lunch came around, Hex was sore all over, and Earth was even closer to being invaded.

"See you in the vid-zone, Hex! We don't want to miss the launch of the first invasion fleet!" shouted Dooper as he unzipped his holo-suit and climbed out.

"Great. . ." whispered Hex, tugging on his zip.

"So, you must have a few bruises under that disguise," said Opo, packing her holo-suit away.

"Yeah, just my luck I suppose," sighed Hex, pulling on the zip with his teeth. "And now I'm stuck in this holo-suit. Perfect! Just perfect! Now, I can't go anywhere without everyone thinking I'm an earthling! That is, if my tele-belt actually teleports me where I want to go. . ."

"You know what I think?" said Opo, putting a sucker on Hex's shoulder. "Maybe one day you'll look back on all this bad luck and realize that it isn't *bad* luck at all. That maybe these things make sense. You know what I mean?"

"You're not the first planetexian to say that. . . but it's hard to believe right now," said Hex, yanking the zip desperately with both earthling hands, as he watched Opo teleport away. A moment later, Glitch poked his head out of Hex's pocket.

"Well, here we are, Glitch – just you and me, stuck in a holo-suit with an unpredictable tele-belt."

"Klik-POP-klik!" said Glitch, sympathetically.

"Oh, and what's more, Earth is only an hour away from being invaded, and I have no plan to save it! Perfect! My dad's going to get disintegrated and there's nothing I . . . can . . . do. . ."

Hex stopped. He looked down at his human-looking hand and then at his tele-belt. After a moment, Hex closed his eyes and made what could only be described as a *wish*. It was a wish to save his dad, one way or another, no matter what. He opened his eyes, turned the tele-belt to receive, and de-materialized.

PERIL AT THE PALACE

It took Hex 3.4 seconds to realize that he hadn't re-materialized at Sporg's School for Space Invaders. He was somewhere quite different. He was now standing in a grand, green hall, with high green walls, green tables and chairs, and ten or fifteen green statues of Empress Valoona dotted around.

"Where am I?" he muttered, wandering to a nearby window. It was a view of New X City that he had never seen before. There seemed to be something not quite right about it, as if one of the landmarks was missing. Hex looked back at a statue of the empress and the planetexian penny dropped.

"It's the empress's palace – I'm in the empress's palace!"

"POP-click!" said Glitch, rolling out of Hex's pocket and on to his shoulder.

"This isn't what I wanted! I have to save my dad – I haven't got time for a tour of the palace!" Hex said to himself, wandering around the gloriously green room. "Stupid Hex Effect!"

Hex turned the dial on his tele-belt again, but nothing happened. He was miles away from the school teleporter – who knew when, if ever, it was going to pick up his signal? He started creeping slowly down the corridor, trying to find a way out. But every time he turned a corner, he was presented with another corridor, lined with statue after statue of the empress.

"POP-klik-klik-POP!" said Glitch, tapping Hex urgently on the shoulder with a tiny arm.

"Shh-hh!" said Hex. "We have to stay quiet. We don't want to alert any—"

"HALT! Don't move, in the name of Her Majestic

Green, the Empress Valoona XIII!" came a cry. Hex spun around to see a green-clad guard wielding a menacing-looking ray-gun.

"YAAAH!" screamed Hex.

"YAAAAAAAAAAAAHHH!" screamed the guard, and ran as fast as he could in the other direction!

"What was that about?" asked Hex.

"Klik-POP! Chik!" said Glitch, shaking his head.

"Scared of me? Why would he be scared of—" began Hex.

"EARTHLING!" came another cry. "There he is!"

Hex turned again. It was the guard, but this time he had brought reinforcements – *more* guards! There must have been ten or eleven. . . Hex looked down at his suckers, and saw earthling hands in their place.

"Oh, no. . ." he muttered. "Glitch! They think I'm an earth—"

ZWAAAARK!

A disintegration ray missed Hex's head by an antenna's breadth, disintegrating a statue of Empress

Valoona! Hex screamed and ran!

"Green alert! An earthling has invaded the palace! Blast him!" shouted one of the guards. A loud siren began blaring as Hex sped down the corridor, through a portal and out on to a moving conveyor! Hex started to run, but he was running the *wrong way* down the conveyor – he was hardly moving! Panicking, he hopped off and ducked through a portal into another zone.

"Death to the earthling invader! Protect the empress!" cried the guards.

"Wait! I can explain!" yelled Hex, as a disintegration beam whizzed past him, destroying another statue of the empress. Hex skidded through another portal, emerging into the biggest zone he had ever seen! It was tall and round, and so high that he could hardly see the ceiling. Balcony after balcony coiled along the walls, with a hundred portals leading to who knew where. The hall was filled to bursting with emerald statues of the empress. In desperation, Hex ducked behind one of the statues as the guards followed him into the zone.

"I've got to get out of this holo-suit!" whispered Hex.

"As long as they think I'm an earthling I'm going to be right at the top of their disintegration list! Glitch, see if you can unstick the zip."

Glitch rolled around to the base of Hex's neck and started tugging on the zip.

"Wait . . . Glitch, stop!" whispered Hex.

"POP? Klik-POP?" asked a confused Glitch.

"Don't you see? They think I'm an earthling! Glitch, this is it! This is my chance to save Dad! All I need to do is find the empress, hope that she doesn't see through my disguise, and persuade her to call off the invasion!"

"Klik-POP! Chik!" said Glitch, doubtfully.

"I know it sounds crazy, but it's the best chance I've got to save Dad. All I need to do is convince the empress that I'm a real, live—"

"EARTHLING!" came a shout. "There he is!"

He'd been spotted! Hex leapt to his feet and started running, as disintegration rays streaked past his hear lobes.

"By the empress's emerald toothbrush, the earthling is escaping!" cried a guard. "Release the sentry-bots!"

"Sentry-bots?" Hex repeated nervously. He was almost at the other end of the zone when he saw two massive portals open in the far wall. A moment later, two huge, floating bucket-shaped robots appeared from inside the portals! They were massive and menacing with enormous pincers and shoulder-mounted ray-guns – none of which was good news for Hex. He stared in horror as the sentry-bots started floating towards him.

"HALT! HALT IN THE NAME OF THE EMPRESS!" cried one of the sentry-bots. Hex tried to dodge out of the way, but he was too slow – the sentry-bot blocked his path and grabbed Hex by the neck! Hex gasped for air as he was lifted up.

"W-wait . . . I c-come in p-peace!" wheezed Hex.

"PEACE! DOES NOT COMPUTE! DEATH TO EARTHLINGS!" said the sentry-bot, and aimed its shoulder ray-guns.

"Klik-POP!" yelled Glitch, and rolled up the sentry-bot's pincer! The little robot zoomed up the sentry-bot's huge bucket-like body, and began whizzing around its head at high speed!

"AAAH! THE EARTHLING HAS RELEASED SOME SORT OF PARASITE! GET IT OFF! GET IT OFF!" cried the sentry-bot, spinning around.

"HOLD STILL!" cried the second sentry-bot, trying to grab the speedy Glitch in its pincers.

The first sentry-bot squealed in panic, and threw Hex into the air! Hex landed squarely on top of the second sentry-bot! Hex grabbed on to an aerial on top of the sentry-bot's head as it tried to shake him loose.

"AAH! THE EARTHLING IS ON ME! IT'S TOUCHING MY SENSOR ARRAY! UNCLEAN! BLAST IT!" cried the second sentry-bot, spinning around. The first sentry-bot fired its ray-guns, trying to blast Hex, but with Glitch zooming all over its view sensors, it could barely see!

ZWAAAAARRRK!

The death ray seared past Hex as he hung on for dear life, but as he was flung from left to right, he spotted something familiar on the back of the sentry-bot's head.

"Control panel. . ." he said. It was an enormous version of the panel on Glitch's head! There could only be one thing underneath – the primary control module!

As the sentry-bot bucked and wheeled to avoid the other robot's death rays, Hex slipped his hand under a small groove at the bottom of the control panel. There was a *clink-clunk!* as the sentry-bot's control panel popped open!

"I did it. . ." cried Hex. He let go of the sentry-bot's antenna, and reached both hands inside its head. He understood the workings of the robot immediately, as if he'd invented it himself. "OK, power cartridge, data bubbles, coupling rods, primary control module! Got it!"

Hex wrapped his fingers around the control module and squeezed. The sentry-bot twitched – Hex had control! He felt his way around the control module, until his hands found the death ray triggers.

"Glitch, get off – now!" cried Hex, tugging on the control module and moving the sentry-bot into position. Glitch popped in panic and hopped off the other sentry-bot.

"OK," said Hex. "My turn."

131

ZWAAAAARKKK!

The death ray streaked across the hall, disintegrating one of the other sentry-bot's shoulder ray-guns, sending the robot spinning into a giant statue of the empress! It ricocheted into a nearby wall and exploded in a shower of sparks!

Hex moved the sentry-bot to swoop down and scoop Glitch up with one of its pincers; then he floated back into the air.

'Klik-POP! Klik," said Glitch, delightedly.

"We did it . . . we actually did it!" said Hex, breathing a heavy sigh of relief. "OK, *now* we find the emp—"

"DIE, earthling!" Hex heard from behind him. It was the planetexian guards! They had already taken aim – there was no time for Hex to react. Disintegration rays streaked towards him!

ZWAAARK! ZWAARK! ZWAARK! ZWAARK!

The beams struck the sentry-bot, blowing off its shoulder ray-guns and half of its armour! The robot lolled in the air and then began spinning towards a nearby wall.

"Glitch, I can't keep it in the air! Hang on to something!" screamed Hex. The sentry-bot whirled towards the wall, faster and closer until. . .

KROOOOM!!

It smashed through the wall, and then bounced along the ground. Hex tried his best to hang on, but the force of the impact threw him across the room! He skidded to a halt, covered in green debris, dust and scorch marks.

"Ow. . ." said Hex, checking to see whether he'd been at all disintegrated. He looked up. He was in a large, green chamber. Its walls were covered with portrait after portrait of the empress. In one corner he could make out what looked like a sink, but the rest of the room was too full of green dust to make out anything else. Hex struggled to his feet, and brushed himself off.

"Glitch? Where are you? Glitch! Are you OK?" he said, looking around. Glitch was nowhere to be seen! He was surely disintegrated, or crushed underneath the—

"Clik-clik-POP!"

Hex looked up. It was Glitch, clinging on to the top of his head.

134

"Glitch!" cried Hex. "You're OK!"

"Klik . . . tsss! Tss!" said Glitch, blowing green dust out of his filters.

"Sorry, Glitch, this didn't exactly turn out as I planned," sighed Hex. "I can't believe I thought I could just wander around until I found the empress, especially looking like an—"

"EARTHLING!" came a high-pitched scream.

Hex spun around. Was it a guard? A sentry-bot? He peered into the far corner of the room. There, in the haze of dust, he could just make out a fat female planetexian sitting on a toilet.

It was the empress!

AN AUDIENCE WITH THE EMPRESS

TIME UNTIL INVASION: 4.6 MINUTES

"AAAAAH! Earthling! Earthling!" screamed the empress, trembling with terror on her emerald toilet. "HELP! The palace has been invaded! Guards! Sentry-bots! Protect me! I'm so very, *very* important!"

"Sorry, I didn't mean to. . ." squeaked a panicking Hex, but Glitch tapped him on the head.

"Chik-tic-POP!"

"What? Oh, yeah! Earthling! Right, right. . ." said Hex, remembering how he looked. He glanced back at the hole in the wall. It wouldn't be long before the guards arrived. Hex had to act fast.

"Um, excuse me, Empress, but the thing is. . ." began Hex, trying to think of something earthling-like to say.

"You've destroyed my royal relief zone! And my sentry-bot! Impossible! No one has ever destroyed my sentry-bots before! I thought you earthlings were just weak-minded mud-creatures – I had no idea what you were capable of! Oh, please don't eat me!" pleaded the empress.

"Eat you?" said Hex, feeling queasy at the thought of it, but when he saw the look of fear in the empress's eyes (and her antenna glowing blue with terror), he steadied himself and said, "Yes, eat you! That's what I'll do! We eat anything, us earthlings! Mud, each other . . . and especially space invaders! And I'd know, because I definitely am one!"

"No, please! I'm Her Majestic Green, the Empress Valoona XIII!" squealed the empress. "There's a whole planet of much less significant planetexians out there . . . and I can bring you as many as you can eat! Just spare me!"

"What? No, that's not what I want! I mean, *we* want! We, the earthlings! We want you to call off the invasion of Earth!" said Hex, loudly.

"Call *off* the invasion? For good? But invading's what we *do*. . ." said the empress, not quite able to get her head around the idea, even in the face of being eaten.

"You have to call it off! Look, there are loads of other planets to invade, why not pick one of them?" asked Hex.

"Well, I suppose," replied the empress. "It's just, well, I'd *really* set my sights on Earth. . ."

"Look, you don't seem to get it! You'd better cancel the invasion of Earth and swear never to invade Earth ever again or you're in big trouble!" bellowed Hex, almost starting to enjoy himself. "I mean, look what I did to your sentry-bot! And that was with one sucker – I mean, hand – tied behind my back!"

"I'm sorry!" cried the empress. "Obviously I would *never* have chosen Earth if I thought you were going have a problem with it!"

"Well, I do! I mean, we do! Because there are loads of us, just waiting to attack! A billion! No, a trillion! No, more! What's more than a trillion?"

"Uh, a squillion?" said the empress, clearly not sure.

"Yeah, a squillion!" repeated Hex. "So unless you want a squillion hungry earthlings on your doorstep—"

"No! All right! All right! I'll call off the invasion! Whatever you say!" said the empress.

"Really? That's great! Thanks so much!" said Hex, as he felt Glitch tapping him hard on the top of his head. He turned around to see the empress's guards clambering through the hole in the royal relief zone wall. He looked back at the empress, who was clearly deciding whether to stick to her promise, or shout "Disintegrate the earthling!", but she never got the

139

chance. Hex's tele-belt had started to rumble and fizzle – it had picked up the teleporter signal!

"I have to go now," said Hex. "But don't forget – leave Earth alone, or we'll put Planet X on the menu . . . and you'll be the first course!"

The last thing Hex saw before he teleported was the empress faint and fall off her toilet.

THE HEX EFFECT

Hex re-materialized back inside training zone 78! He immediately checked that he and Glitch were in one piece.

"Did . . . did that just happen? I mean, did we really just do that?" said Hex, not quite able to believe it.

"Chik-klik-POP!" replied Glitch, happily.

"I can't wait to tell. . . Dad!" he said, unclipping his P.A.D. from his belt. "Dad? Are you there?"

> HEX! ARE YOU OK, SON? HAS
> ANYTHING HAPPENED?

"Hi Dad! Uh, I'll tell you later," said Hex. "Let's just say I think the empress has changed her mind about invading Earth. . ."

YOU DID IT? I KNEW YOU WOULD! YOU SEE? I TOLD YOU TO TRUST IN THE HEX EFFECT! JUST WAIT TILL YOU GET HERE – I HAVE SO MUCH TO TEACH YOU. . .

"But how? How do I get to Earth?" asked Hex.

WELL, THERE MIGHT BE A BLACK HOLE OR TWO TO GET THROUGH . . . BUT NOTHING YOU CAN'T HANDLE! AND DON'T FORGET – I'LL BE RIGHT HERE ON YOUR P.A.D. IF YOU NEED ME BEFORE THEN.

"Actually, there is one thing," said Hex, staring at one of his disguised suckers. "You don't know how to fix a stuck holo-suit zip, do you?"

TRY TWISTING IT FIRST. THAT ALWAYS WORKS FOR ME.

Hex gave the zip a twist, and it came unstuck! He clambered out of the holo-suit, delighted to be looking himself again. "It worked!" he whooped.

Hex rushed down the corridor and into the vid-zone, where the entire school had gathered to see the empress signal the invasion. He scrambled through the gathered pupils until he found Roswell class, and then shuffled in beside Dooper.

"Hey, Hex – you made it just in time!" said Dooper, his antenna glowing orange with excitement. "Can you believe it? The invasion is actually happening!"

Hex didn't reply. He just took a deep breath and wondered whether the empress would keep her word after all.

"ATTENTION CITIZENS OF PLANET X! HER MAJESTIC GREEN, THE EMPRESS VALOONA, IS ABOUT TO ADDRESS HER PEOPLE!"

The empress's fat face appeared on the giant holo-screen, and a cheer went up from the whole school.

"Loyal citizens of Planet X," began the empress, sheepishly. "I know how you have all been looking forward to the invasion, which was due to start in less than a minute. However, after much wise, empress-like consideration – and with no outside influences whatsoever – I have decided to *cancel* the invasion of Earth!"

The whole of Sporg's School for Space Invaders seemed to groan in unison! Except Hex, who grinned from hear lobe to hear lobe.

"It has come to my attention that there are much better, more, um . . . invade-able planets out there! Earth isn't good enough to be the next Planet X! I shall pick another planet – a better planet, a planet that will fall before the might of the glorious planetexian army! Tune in for the live final, two weeks from now!"

Another cheer went up from the crowd.

Even Hex cheered – he'd done it! He'd stopped the invasion of Earth! What's more, one way or another, it was all down to the Hex Effect. Then, through the growing noise from the invasion-hungry pupils, Hex heard a familiar voice.

"So, you managed to get out of the holo-suit, then?"

Hex turned to see Opo smiling back at him.

"Yeah, you just have to twist the zip," replied Hex.

"Do not think for a moment this means your training will stop!" shouted Headmaster Sporg. "There's still plenty to learn, and plenty of planets left to invade! But for now, fill up on gloop – it's lunchtime! Set your tele-belts to 'receive' and prepare to be transported to the ingestion zone!"

As everyone turned their tele-belt dials, Hex turned to Opo. "Can I ask you something? After you found my burnt holo-badge, why didn't you tell anyone it was me in the hypersaucer?"

Opo smiled. "Do you think you're the only planetexian who doesn't want to be a space invader? There are *loads* of us."

"There . . . there are?" asked Hex.

"You'll see," said Opo. "You never know; that luck of yours might be looking up."

"Yeah – maybe it is!" said Hex, as he watched Opo vanish. He turned his tele-belt to "receive" and de-materialized. A second later, he re-materialized in the ingestion zone . . . right in the middle of the Big Gloop Bowl! As the gloop tube opened above his head, he looked up.

"Or maybe not. . ." he sighed.

S l o o o o o o o o o o o o o o o r r r t !

ALIEN ESCAPE

DISINTEGRATE FOR VICTORY!

JOIN THE INVASION EFFORT AND HELP DISINTEGRATE THE ENEMIES OF PLANET X!

(ANYONE NOT JOINING THE EFFORT WILL BE DISINTEGRATED.)

THE GREAT GREEN HALL

The Great Green Hall was filled to bursting. Hex had never seen so many planetexians in one place before! But why were they all there? And, more importantly, what was *he* doing there?

"Move!" said a voice behind him. Hex looked back to see two planetexian guards, dressed in impressive silver and green uniforms. Without warning, one of them jabbed him in the back with an electric prod-rod.

"Yow!" said Hex, stumbling forward. His eyes darted nervously around the gathered planetexians. There, in the crowd, was his mother, looking very disappointed.

Soon, Hex spotted more familiar faces – his friends from school, Dooper and Opo, and even Opo's unbearable brother, Steek, looking thoroughly smug.

Hex tried desperately to remember how he'd got into this mess. A moment later, he caught sight of a fat planetexian at the end of the hall. She was sitting on a grand, floating throne, with an ornate crown pushed tightly over her enormous brain-sack.

It was the empress.

"Her Majestic Green, the Empress Valoona XIII!" came a cry. At once, the crowd fell to their knees and bowed deeply. Everyone except Hex. He was frozen to the spot, unable to move, as the empress floated towards him on her gravity-defying throne. Hex held his gill-breath as the empress's third eye opened and inspected him closely.

"Hex-37," she snarled, her telepathy nodes pulsing. "We meet at last."

"Uh, hi," whimpered Hex, meekly waving a sucker.

"You have been accused of the most un-green treachery," hissed the empress. "You have betrayed your people, you have betrayed your planet, and you have betrayed your family and friends! But worst of all, you have betrayed . . . me!"

"No, please, it's not like that. I just wanted to help my dad!" Hex cried. "It's all the Hex Effect's fault!"

"This is my planet – mine!" snarled the empress. "All I've ever asked from you is a little space invading. Is that too much to expect? You are a planetexian, aren't you? And what do planetexians love?"

"SPACE INVADING!" shouted the crowd.

"Exactly! But not you – oh no, *you* had to be different!" barked the empress. "Well different won't do, not on my planet! For we all know that difference leads to. . ."

"DISINTEGRATION!" yelled the gathered planetexians.

The empress pointed a sucker into the air, and Hex looked up to see three huge sentry-bots float down from the ceiling. Hex screamed, but he was drowned out by chants of "DISINTEGRATE! DISINTEGRATE!".

The empress smiled. "Goodbye, Hex," she said, "and good morning!"

Good morning? thought Hex, as the sentry-bots took aim.

ZWAAARK!

"NooOOOoo!" screamed Hex, sitting bolt upright and bashing his antenna on the top of his slumber pod. It was a dream! Hex rubbed his eyes and checked that he had all his suckers and gills, nervous green sweat running down his forehead.

"I *said*, good morning!" said T.K.421, the computer that operated Hex's hover-home in the skies just outside New X City. A robotic pincer snaked out of the wall and pulled off Hex's sheet. "Time to get up! It's another beautiful day on Planet X! The suns are shining, radiation levels are just above tolerable and there's only a 26.6 per cent chance of acid rain! So, are you looking forward to another day of space invader training?"

"Can't wait. Look, would you give me a few minutes, T.K.?" said Hex, as the robotic pincer tried to lift Hex out of the slumber pod by his ankle.

"Three minutes! You don't want your breakfast to go cold – gloop is best served lukewarm!" said T.K.

Hex slumped back on to the bed, and a small, round robot rolled out from under his pillow.

"Pinch me, Glitch," said Hex. "Just to make sure I'm not still dreaming."

Hex's friend (and his best invention to date) stared at his green-skinned companion in confusion. "Click-POP?" Glitch asked.

"Of course I'm serious," said Hex.

Glitch shrugged, reached out a tiny robotic arm and pinched Hex on the sucker.

"Ow! Thanks," said Hex. "I needed that."

"Kik-kik-POP-POP?" asked Glitch.

"Yeah, another nightmare, the same as all the others," sighed Hex. "It's like I'm on trial or something, for tricking the empress into calling off the invasion of Earth. And then just as I'm about to get disintegrated, I wake up."

Only a week ago, Hex-37 had single-suckeredly prevented the invasion of a muddy little planet called Earth. It wasn't that he particularly cared about saving the earthlings – after all, he was used to Planet X conquering world after world. It was all planetexians ever did, or seemed to think about. But Hex had found out that his *father* was on Earth, and that had changed everything.

Hex had always thought his dad had been lost in space during a routine hypersaucer lesson, but in truth (and by sheer bad luck), his dad had ended up on the same world that Planet X was preparing to invade. Hex knew then that he had to try and save his father, but he had no idea how.

Hex still couldn't understand how he'd succeeded – how he'd found himself disguised as an earthling, or how he'd teleported to the royal palace and scared the empress into cancelling the invasion. There was only one explanation for all the strange things that had happened – a family curse known as the "Hex Effect".

Whether it was good luck or bad, from the moment Hex had started space invader training, the Hex Effect had changed his life for ever. Despite being years ahead of his classmates when it came to technology and robotics, Hex had the worst luck with anything to do with space invading. Ray-guns, hypersaucers – you name it. They would all suddenly malfunction. It had been the same for Hex's dad, and his dad before him, and so on, for thirty-six generations – as soon as the Hexes started space invader training, anything that could go wrong, did go wrong.

PING! PING!

Hex reached over to his bedside table and picked up his Personal Advice Device. "Dad?" he said.

Hex waited a moment, staring at the small, silver object resting in his sucker. Not only did his P.A.D. contain a constantly updated database of *Everything you need to know about Space Invading, but were afraid to ask*, but it was the only way his father could contact him from Earth.

MORNING, SON. DID YOU SLEEP WELL?

"I'm still not completely sure I've woken up," replied Hex, rubbing his huge, oval eyes.

ANOTHER NIGHTMARE?

"Half the time I can't sleep, and the rest of the time I have nightmares!" groaned Hex. "I just can't shake the feeling that someone's going to find out what I did."

EVERYTHING IS GOING TO BE OK, SON. THERE'S NO WAY

> THE EMPRESS COULD KNOW IT WAS YOU UNDERNEATH THAT EARTHLING DISGUISE.

"But how can you be sure? What if she's realized I wasn't a real earthling? What if she sends her guards to get me . . . or her sentry-bots?" said Hex, working himself into a green lather.

> BUT SHE HASN'T, HEX. BELIEVE ME, IT'S GOING TO BE FINE. THE ONLY WAY ANYONE IS GOING TO FIND OUT WHAT YOU DID IS IF YOU ACTUALLY CONFESS, AND THERE'S NO WAY THAT'S NOT GOING TO HAPPEN, IS THERE?

"No way . . . I'm keeping my mouth and telepathy nodes shut. I haven't even told Mum," said Hex.

> I THINK WE BOTH KNOW THAT'S FOR THE BEST. I THINK YOUR MOTHER'S THE LAST PERSON YOU SHOULD TELL ABOUT YOUR LITTLE ADVENTURE. I CAN JUST IMAGINE HOW MUCH SHE WAS LOOKING FORWARD TO INVADING EARTH.

"Yeah, she was pretty excited," sighed Hex.

IN FACT, IT'S BEST THAT NO ONE – ESPECIALLY YOUR
MUM – FINDS OUT ABOUT ME. YOU SHOULD MAKE SURE
YOU DELETE MY MESSAGES FROM YOUR P.A.D. INBOX.
YOU DON'T WANT ANYONE CHECKING IT WHILE
YOU'RE NOT LOOKING.

"OK, Dad," said Hex, sadly. As great as it was to know
that his dad was alive, it made Hex wish he could trust
his mum with his secret. But Hex knew she put space
invading before anything else. After all, everyone on
Planet X did.

SO, HAVE YOU THOUGHT ANY MORE ABOUT COMING
TO EARTH? THE SOONER YOU'RE AWAY FROM PLANET X,
THE BETTER.

"Uh, I have to go, Dad . . . I'm late for school," said
Hex. "I'll talk to you at lunchtime, OK?"

He turned off the P.A.D. quickly. It wasn't that he

didn't want to escape to Earth – he would give anything to get off Planet X, especially now. Plus his dad made Earth sound very appealing, even if they did only have one sun. But Hex was so scared of being found out that the idea of trying to escape filled him with dread.

Hex was about to delete his dad's messages from his P.A.D. when a robotic pincer grabbed him by the ankle and dragged him out of his slumber pod.

"Three minutes are up!" said T.K.421. "You've got a long and glorious day of space invading ahead of you!"

HEX'S PRESENT

Once washed, scrubbed and dressed in his silver uniform, complete with his unpredictable, ancient tele-belt (the Hex Effect had destroyed his first one), Hex slipped Glitch into his pocket and stepped on the conveyor belt. He was immediately whisked into the ingestion zone for breakfast.

"DIE, ALIEN SCUM!" cried his mother, pointing a ray-gun right in his face!

"Waaaaaaaah!" screamed Hex and dived on to the ground.

"Sorry, just practising . . . honestly, Hex, you've been

so jumpy lately," said his mother, spinning the ray-gun around her sucker. "I just wanted to show you your new present."

"Pr-present?" said Hex, nervously. Hex's mother held out her sucker and handed Hex the ray-gun.

"A ray-gun?" said Hex, staring worriedly at the red, oval-shaped pistol. Any other planetexian would have been pleased with such an impressive present, but the Hex Effect had a way of making sure nothing worked as it was supposed to.

"I know it's not your hatching day for another month or so, but since the empress called off the attack on

Planet Earth, I thought you could do with some fun!" she said. As captain of the 101st hypersaucer fleet, Hex's mother was one of the best space invaders on Planet X. Hex had never met anyone who loved space invading so much – the only time she was really happy was when she was blowing things up.

"Thanks, Mum," he said, forcing a smile as he clipped the ray-gun to his tele-belt. "It's . . . it's just what I wanted."

"Oh good, I hoped you'd like it," said his mother, putting a sucker on his shoulder. "You know what they say, a space invader without a ray-gun is like a nudlork without puss-ducts."

"Uh, did my replacement tele-belt arrive? I still can't seem to fix this one," asked Hex. "I was teleported to the wrong training zone six times last week. I don't even have to turn it on any more – once it teleported me on to the school roof in the middle of a lesson! I mean it did get me out of crop circle training, but. . ."

"Sorry, Hex, you'll have to put up with it for a while. There's been a delay at the factory. All production has halted until the empress's new project is finished – some sort of new *super* sentry-bot," said his mum, turning on the news-vid.

QUESTION: WHAT'S MORE SUPER THAN A SENTRY-BOT? ANSWER: A SUPER SENTRY-BOT!

"Following the recent attack on New X City by the pathetic, mud-sucking earthlings who aren't even worth invading anyway, Her Majestic Green, the Empress Valoona XIII, has ordered the construction of the *ultimate* planetary protector – a super sentry-bot, capable of repelling any invader and crushing any enemy!"

A picture of an enormous robot appeared on the vid-screen. It looked very much like the sentry-bots Hex had encountered on his "accidental" trip to the empress's palace, with a massive, bucket-shaped body, immense shoulder-mounted ray-cannons and sharp, metal pincers. But this robot was *huge*, at least three times bigger than a hypersaucer! It was easily the most impressive thing Hex had ever seen and made his own robotic creations pale in comparison.

"Amazing," he whispered.

"Klik-ka-chik-kik!" huffed Glitch, jealously, from Hex's pocket.

"Sorry, Glitch. You know you're still my number one bot," whispered Hex.

"What?" asked his mother.

"I said, uh, it looks like it couldn't be stopped!" replied Hex, pushing Glitch back in his pocket. Hex knew how much his mum hated his robot-making hobby, and did his best to keep Glitch hidden.

"It certainly does. How generous of the empress to provide us with a global guardian – no one will dare attack us again!" said Hex's mum.

Hex bit his lip. He could never tell his mum that he was

the one who had "attacked" New X City in a hypersaucer –
yet another accident caused by the Hex Effect.

"Two minutes till the skybus arrives! Eat up, Hex!"
said T.K., placing two bowls of gloop on the table. Hex
scrunched his face up. Gloop was the only food on
Planet X and Hex hated it at the best of times. Today,
with a belly full of nerves, he began to feel more than a
little queasy. He pushed the gloop bowl aside and made
his way to the ejection chute. As he was launched on to
the waiting platform, he took out his P.A.D. again, and
turned it on. He leant into the P.A.D. and whispered, "I
want to get away."

There was a pause.

IT SOUNDS LIKE YOU WANT TO ESCAPE FROM
PLANET X. IS THIS TRUE? IF SO, PLEASE
SAY YES . . .

. . . AND THE PLANETEXIAN POLICE WILL BE
WITH YOU IN A FEW MOMENTS TO ARREST YOU
AND TAKE YOU DIRECTLY TO YOUR NEAREST
DISINTEGRATION CHAMBER.

IF THIS IS NOT TRUE, PLEASE SAY NO.

"No! No, it's not true! I don't want to escape! Everything's fine!" shrieked Hex and quickly turned off his P.A.D. That settled it. There was no way he was trying to escape – it was just too risky. Before long, the skybus appeared in the distance, snaking across the pink planetexian sky. Hex sloped on, hoping that he could make it through one day at Sporg's School for Space Invaders without anything bad happening.

"BOOM!"

MIND-CONTROL TRAINING

At the sound of the **"BOOM!"** Hex let out a panicked yelp and threw himself to the floor of the skybus . . . but then immediately realized it was just his friend, Dooper (the biggest boy in his class by a good antenna's length), getting excited about blowing things up. The other children (and even the skybus driver) started laughing at Hex, and didn't stop till he shuffled into the seat next to Dooper.

"Hey, Hex! I was just telling everyone about my trip to the Disintegration Range this weekend. I disintegrated fifty-eight target-bots – in thirty-nine

169

seconds! It was a new record! BOOM! **BOOM!**" he bellowed, blowing the end of his suckers as if they were ray-gun barrels.

"Uh, is there any way we could not talk about disintegration, just for today?" asked Hex.

"Are you OK, Hex?" said Opo, leaning over the seat in front of him. "You look like you haven't slept in a week."

"I wish I hadn't," said Hex, rubbing his tired eyes and attempting a smile.

If anyone might understand about his predicament, it would be Opo. She was the only other creature on Planet X who knew that it was Hex who had accidentally attacked New X City during hypersaucer training, and she hadn't told anyone about it.

But what if she found out he had deliberately made the empress call off the invasion of Earth? Even if she wasn't the biggest fan of space invading, would she really betray the empress? Hex couldn't risk trusting her – or anyone else. As far as he was concerned, honesty could only lead to one thing – disintegration.

"What's the matter, Hex-37? Is the training too much for you?" sneered Steek from across the aisle. Opo's twin brother was the one planetexian (apart from the empress) that Hex would be happy never to see again.

"Face facts," Steek continued, "you Hexes just aren't cut out for space invading."

"Shut your gills, *Stink*! Team Dooper and Hex will be blowing stuff up before you even finish your first year!" bellowed Dooper.

"I wasn't talking to you, *Dopey*. Why don't you keep your antenna out of my face, you big, fat bowl of gloop," snarled Steek.

"I've already told you, I'm not fat! I have overactive elbow glands!" protested Dooper.

"Ignore him, Hex," said Opo. "The thing you have to remember about my brother is he doesn't know how to be anything other than a pain in the nodes. . ."

"Hey, is that a ray-gun?" said Steek, spotting Hex's present clipped to his tele-belt. "Who on Planet X thought it was a good idea to give *you* a ray-gun?"

171

"My, uh, my mum bought it for me," replied Hex, quietly.

"What was she thinking?" said Steek. "Doesn't she know about the Hex Effect? You're the last person on Planet X who should have a ray-gun! Knowing you, you'll end up disintegrating someone . . . or yourself!"

Steek continued to prod and pester Hex about being disintegrated all the way to Sporg's School for Space Invaders. By the time they arrived, Hex's nerves were more shredded than ever.

The children herded into the school, and then Hex and the rest of Roswell class teleported to training zone 13, where their teacher, Miss Voob, was waiting for them.

As Hex materialized in the training zone, he was grateful that at least his tele-belt seemed to be working today. For a moment, Hex wondered if the Hex Effect had actually worn off.

"Pay attention, Roswell class," said Miss Voob. "Today we are going to be learning about mind-control, a vital tool in any invader's arsenal."

The class saw the blue glow of teleportation energy

172

appear in the middle of the zone. A second later, a green box appeared on Miss Voob's desk. She opened it and took out a silver, bowl-shaped contraption. "This is a *minding module*," she continued. "It will allow you to read thoughts, befuddle your enemies, and even command them to do your—"

"MISS VOOB, REPORT IMMEDIATELY TO TRAINING ZONE 51. CLASS SUPERVISION REQUIRED IN TRAINING ZONE 51," said a voice over the tannoy.

"Oh, for goodness' sake . . . where are the assisto-bots when you need them?" moaned Miss Voob. "Honestly, it's all very well the school's bots helping to build the empress's new super sentry-bot, but I'm left running around like a blue-bottomed beezle! Right, I'll be five minutes – who can I trust with the minding module until then?"

"Pick me! Pick me!" cried Steek. "I'm responsible!"

"Ah, Steek – eager as ever," smiled Miss Voob as she handed Steek the minding module. "In the meantime, everyone take out your P.A.D.s and find out all you can about how to use the minding module."

As Miss Voob de-materialized and Steek proudly cradled the minding module, everyone unclipped their P.A.D.s from their belts and turned them on. Hex sighed and mumbled "minding module" into his P.A.D.

PING!

IT LOOKS LIKE YOU ARE TRYING TO BE TELEPATHIC. CAN I HELP?

"Telepathic?" whispered Hex, nervous of what was coming next.

INVADING CAN BE A TRICKY BUSINESS. YOU MIGHT FIND YOURSELF ON A STRANGE PLANET, FULL OF CREATURES THAT DO NOT SPEAK YOUR LANGUAGE, AND WHO ARE NOT TOO KEEN ON BEING INVADED. NO PROBLEM! WITH THE MINDING MODULE YOU CAN FIND OUT EVERYTHING YOU NEED TO KNOW FROM THEM, AND GET THEM TO DO WHAT YOU WANT, WITHOUT EVEN RAISING A SUCKER. WHY DISINTEGRATE YOUR ENEMY, WHEN YOU CAN

GET THEM TO DISINTEGRATE THEMSELVES? HERE IS HOW IT WORKS:

ATTACH THE MINDING MODULE TO YOUR TELEPATHY NODES

CHOOSE FROM ONE OF THE TWO SETTINGS:
● CONTROL - ALLOWS YOU TO CONTROL YOUR VICTIM'S EVERY MOVE!
● PROBE — READ YOUR ENEMY'S THOUGHTS! ● AND THEN AWAY YOU THINK!

*PLEASE NOTE: RANGE LIMITED. NATURAL RESISTANCE TO MIND-CONTROL MAY AFFECT RESULTS. ALWAYS READ THE INSTRUCTIONS. PLANET X ACCEPTS NO RESPONSIBILITY FOR BRAIN DRAIN DUE TO IMPROPER USE.

"*Mind-reading?*" whispered Hex, frantically. "I can't have my mind read!"

"Chik! POP!" said Glitch in agreement, poking his head out of Hex's pocket.

"Right, let's get started," said Steek, fixing the minding module to his telepathy nodes.

"I don't think we should be messing around with that thing," said Hex, nervously. "What if something went wrong?"

"I couldn't agree more . . . which is exactly why only *I* will be using it," said Steek, and turned the dial to CONTROL.

"Don't worry, Hex – Stink couldn't control a nudlork, and they don't even *have* brains!" whispered Dooper to Hex, but Dooper's whispers were always loud enough for the whole class to hear.

"You fat gwirm, you can't talk about me like that!" snarled Steek, pointing the minding module at Dooper.

"Hey, my head feels fuzzy, no, fizzy, no, squelchy. . ." said Dooper, grabbing his brain-sack. "What's going –" began Dooper, and then suddenly froze.

"Dooper, are you OK?" asked Hex. Dooper stood still for a moment and then turned to Hex – a strange, blank look in his eyes.

"I am a fat gwirm. I smell like a scum-bug and I live in the spit-pools of swamp gulpers, because I am stupider than a skeeble's armpit and twice as ugly," said

Dooper, his eyes glazed. "Oh, and I *don't* have overactive elbow glands, I just like to stuff my face with gloop! I'm a stupid fat gloop-head!"

Dooper started waving his arms about like a hungry gwirm and jumping up and down. Steek was controlling him! The other children started laughing as Dooper hopped around the zone on one foot, shouting, "Gloop-head! Gloop-head! I'm a stupid gloop-head!"

"Look at him go!" laughed Steek.

"Knock it off, Steek!" shouted Hex.

"Hex is right, Steek – that's enough!" said Opo.

"Sorry, Hex, but Miss Voob left *me* in charge, not you," grinned Steek, making Dooper run face first into a wall!

"Leave him alone!" said Hex, trying to grab the minding module off Steek's head.

"Get off me! You don't know who you're messing with. . ." said Steek, and Hex suddenly felt huge suckers grab him by the shoulders and lift him into the air. It was Dooper, still firmly under Steek's control.

"You're a super stupid gloop-head too, Hex!" said Dooper, clutching Hex in a vice-like grip. "Team Dooper and Hex, the super stupid gloop-head team. Let's do the stupid gloop-head team dance!"

Dooper started dancing Hex around the zone! He

spun him around by his suckers, lifting him into the air!

"S-stop, Dooper – I mean Steek!" cried Hex.

"POP! POP!" said Glitch, falling out of Hex's pocket.

"Ha! Don't they make a lovely couple? Dance, you gloop-heads, dance!" laughed Steek. Then he noticed the ray-gun on Hex's tele-belt. He grinned and commanded Dooper to grab it. Dooper let go of Hex, who went flying into a wall! Hex rubbed his sore brain-sack and then looked up. Dooper was pointing the ray-gun right at him.

"It'd be so easy to put you out of your misery," whispered Steek. "You never know, I might get a medal for services to the empress. . ."

"You . . . you wouldn't!" said Hex.

"Wouldn't I?" hissed Steek.

KRUMP!

Opo leapt on Steek, pushing him face first into the ground! She tried to pull the minding module off his head, but he was wriggling too much for her to grab hold of it. Finally, she managed to turn the minding module dial from CONTROL to PROBE.

"There," she said, pinning him to the ground. "You should be controlling yourself, not anyone else. Now behave, or I'll feed you your magna-boots again!"

"Get off me!" screamed Steek. "I'm in charge! You're breaking school rules!"

"What . . . what happened?" said a confused Dooper. "My brain feels floppy, no, squishy, no, crunchy. . ." A moment later he looked down at his suckers. "Hey, cool, I've got a ray-gun! BOOM!"

"Maybe you should keep it. It suits you more than me, anyway," said Hex, as he felt a little dizzy himself.

"What the – what's going on?" muttered Hex, grabbing his head. After a moment, he spotted Steek, glaring at him. Hex slowly realized what was happening – Steek was trying to read his mind! It felt as if his thoughts were being sucked out of his brain! And they were all secret thoughts!

Disintegration! Hypersaucers! Mindless violence! thought Hex, trying to fill his head with space-invader-related thoughts, but they just reminded him of his secrets!

"It's working!" cried Steek, finally managing to throw Opo off him. He got to his feet and began striding towards Hex. "I'm reading his mind! I'm . . . wait a minute, what – YOW-OW-oW!"

Suddenly Steek was hopping from foot to foot, trying to prise the module from his head as sparks and smoke filled the air! "Get it off! Get it off!"

The gathered children tried to stifle their giggles. Finally, Steek managed to tear the minding module off his head and threw it to the ground. A few good stamps later and it was lying in pieces.

Hex couldn't believe it. Could it have been the Hex Effect? It had never worked in his favour before – at least not directly. For a moment, Hex wondered if things were looking up.

But only for a moment.

"What in the name of the empress's emerald underwear is going on here?" said Miss Voob, re-materializing in the training zone. "Steek, are you all right? Why is there smoke coming off your brain-sack?"

"Dad . . . alive . . . Dad. . ." Steek said, clutching his head. Hex froze in horror.

"'Dad? Whose dad? You're not making any sense, Steek," said Miss Voob.

"I read his mind!" cried Steek. "Hex's dad is alive . . . on Earth!"

SECRETS AND LIES
(AND SPACE INVASION)

"No, no, no," said Miss Voob, as Roswell class gathered around. "I'm afraid Hex's dad isn't the least bit alive – he was sucked into a black hole. Isn't that right, Hex?"

"What? Oh yes! Absolutely!" agreed Hex, quickly.

"It's not true! I mean, yes, he was sucked into a black – look, that's not the point!" cried Steek. "I saw it in my head, just before the minding module blew up! Hex is lying! His dad's alive and well . . . and living on that stinking mudball, Earth!"

"Earth? *Planet* Earth? What are you talking about?

Hex, did Steek read your mind? Is any of this true?" asked Miss Voob, firmly.

Hex panicked. This was it – he'd been found out! He looked around for an escape route, but there was nowhere to run. He reached down to his tele-belt. Maybe if he turned it on it would pick up some random signal and teleport him to the other side of Planet X!

"Excuse me, Miss Voob, but it's my brother who's lying," said Opo. "Steek would do *anything* to get Hex into trouble."

"Yeah, Stink hates Hex!" bellowed Dooper. "He treats him like a glob of gloop on his magna-boot!"

"What? I'm not lying! It's that mucus-spewing slurm-slug who's lying! I read his mind! And there's more . . . I just can't – I just can't get it straight in my head," said Steek, rubbing his telepathy nodes.

"You're such a greeny-meanie!" said Opo, firmly. "Of *course* Hex wishes his dad was still alive. Don't you wish the same about Mum?"

"What? Well yes, but it's not a wish, it's—" began Steek.

"So maybe if you could stop being such a mean old gwirm for two seconds, you'd see how bad it makes Hex feel," said Opo, prodding Steek with a sucker.

"No, that's not the point! Hex is—" tried Steek, but Miss Voob put a sucker on his shoulder.

"I think I've heard enough," she said. "I'm disappointed in you, Steek-55. I thought you were going to look after the minding module responsibly, not use it to make trouble for your fellow invaders."

"But, Miss Voob, it's true! Everyone knows Hex is bad luck! And now we know he's hiding something!"

"I said that's *enough*, Steek-55. Unless you want me to put you on gloop mixing duty. Now it's nearly break time. Everyone teleport down to the recreation zone before I lose my temper."

Hex found his way to the recreation zone in the end, although his tele-belt transported him to the relief zone, ingestion zone and the library before he finally managed to pick up the right signal. He spotted Opo and Dooper in a corner, and made his way over.

"Hex, you made it!" shouted Dooper. "Where have you been? Break's almost over!"

"Just a little tele-belt trouble . . . I've been all over the place. This thing does what it wants."

"Well, thanks for helping me out back there," said Dooper, and then turned an embarrassed shade of green. "Opo was just telling me what I did – in front of *everyone*. . ."

"Actually, you're a pretty good dancer!" joked Hex. "But . . . thanks for helping me, too – both of you. I really appreciate it."

"Believe me, it was my pleasure," said Opo, clenching her suckers.

"Well, it meant a lot," said Hex. "I know it doesn't do much for your popularity. I'm pretty much a joke around here, what with the Hex Effect and everything."

"Don't be silly, we *have* to stick together – we're the same," said Opo.

"We are?" said Hex.

"You bet!" bellowed Dooper. "Wait, how?"

"Look, I lost my mum in the invasion of the last Planet

186

X," said Opo. "I know how hard it is. My brother's always been a pain in the nodes, but he had no right to make up stories about your dad. And it was especially horrid – even for him – to try and get your hopes up like that."

"Stink's a great big gwirm!" said Dooper. "I was a hatchling when I lost my mum and dad. I don't even remember them, but if someone said bad things about them – BOOM! They'd get a sucker sandwich right in the gills!"

Hex suddenly wondered if his friends might understand why he had to save his dad, even if it meant stopping the invasion of Earth.

Opo had already told Hex that she wasn't a fan of space invading, and they'd both lost so much because of it – much more than him. How much could they really like space invading, if it had cost them their parents?

"Hey, do you two want to come over to the orphanarium after school?" Dooper continued. "I've never had friends round before! We'll have the best time ever! We can play alien-in-the-middle and abduction and seek . . . and space invasers! Team Dooper, Hex and Opo, the best space invasers ever! BOOM!"

"BOOM!" shouted Opo with a giggle.

Hex's circulatory organ sank. In the end, everything came back to space invading. Planetexians put space invading before *anything* – even families and friendship.

"Actually, um, I'm a bit busy tonight. Space invader stuff, you know how it is. Maybe another time," said Hex. He suddenly felt rather alone. At least his secret was safe, for now. But Hex knew it was only a matter of time before something else went horribly wrong.

Hex had to work out a plan of action, and there was only one planetexian who could help him now – his dad.

FOUND OUT

The rest of the morning passed without any other problems. Hex was so relieved that no one believed Steek that he didn't even mind a whole hour of abduction training. Even the Hex Effect seemed to be helping for a change – instead of teleporting him to the ingestion zone, he was transported to a quiet corridor – the perfect place to contact his dad in secret.

Hex checked no one was around and took his little robot out of his pocket.

"Keep watch for me, Glitch," he said, and Glitch

rolled on to the floor with a "POP! POP!" Hex took a deep breath and turned on his P.A.D.

PING!

"Dad, are you there?"

There was a pause . . . then:

HI, SON. HOW'S SCHOOL? TROUBLE-FREE, I HOPE?

"Not exactly – I just had my mind read by the meanest boy in the whole school! He knows you're alive!"

MINDING MODULES, I'LL BET. I ALWAYS HATED THOSE THINGS. WHAT ELSE DID HE FIND OUT? DOES ANYONE ELSE SUSPECT ANYTHING?

"Well no, I don't think so. The minding module blew up before he could read any more of my thoughts, but—"

SEE, I TOLD YOU THE HEX EFFECT WOULD COME IN HANDY. IT DOESN'T ALWAYS MESS THINGS UP. . .

"But it's only a matter of time! You're right, Dad – I can't stay here. I have to get off this stupid, invasion-obsessed planet before it's too late!"

YOU'RE MAKING A BRAVE CHOICE, SON, AND IN THE END, YOU'LL SEE THAT IT'S THE RIGHT ONE. EVERYTHING'S GOING TO BE FINE, MARK MY WORDS. WHEN YOU'RE SITTING HERE WITH LEMONADE AND CAKE, YOU'LL LOOK BACK AND REALIZE HOW LUCKY YOU ARE.

"I have no idea what you just said," said Hex. "What's lem and aiden-cake?"

UH, NEVER MIND, LET'S NOT GET OFF THE POINT. FIRST THINGS FIRST – YOU NEED A HYPERSAUCER.

"A *hypersaucer*? Where am I going to get one of those? They won't let us fly real hypersaucers! I mean, I know I *did* fly one, but that was all the Hex Effect's fault."

BELIEVE ME, HEX, AFTER TWENTY-TWO YEARS AT SPORG'S, I THOUGHT THE HEX EFFECT WAS TO BLAME TOO. BUT IN THE END, THAT'S WHAT BROUGHT ME TO EARTH, SAFE AND SOUND. NOW I HAVE A WHOLE NEW LIFE, FREE OF SPACE INVADING AND DISINTEGRATION.

"But I can't wait twenty-two years – I have to get out of here now!" said Hex.

YOUR MOTHER IS A HYPERSAUCER CAPTAIN, SHE MUST HAVE ACCESS TO THE HYPERSAUCER HANGARS. DO YOU THINK YOU COULD CONVINCE HER TO TAKE YOU ON A TOUR?

"Well . . . maybe, but what do I do when I get there? Mum's not going to just let me borrow a hypersaucer!" replied Hex.

YOU'RE PROBABLY RIGHT . . . I KNOW YOU'LL FIND A WAY – EVEN IF IT MEANS STEALING A HYPERSAUCER FROM THE

EMPRESS HERSELF! I WISH I COULD HELP YOU MORE. TRUST IN THE HEX EFFECT, SON. I KNOW YOU DON'T BELIEVE IT NOW, BUT IT'S THE BEST CHANCE YOU HAVE.

"How can I trust it? It's been nothing but trouble ever since I started space invader school! I almost got disintegrated *again* today! Do you know how close Steek got to finding out what I did? I mean, I invaded the royal palace! I smashed up the empress's sentry-bots! I pretended to be an earthling! And then, to top it all off, I made the empress call off the invasion of Earth – while she was sitting on the toilet! What am I supposed to do if someone finds out?" cried Hex.

"Klik-kik-kik POP! POP! POP!" said Glitch, loudly. Hex turned slowly around to see him pointing to the right. There was Opo, standing in the corridor. She'd heard every word he'd said.

"Steek was right – he was right all along. . ." she said, quietly.

"Opo. . . I. . . I—" began Hex, but how could he

possibly explain? Hex panicked, and did the first thing he could think of – he ran!

"Stop! Hex, stop!" cried Opo, chasing after Hex as he raced away. Hex ran as fast as his little green legs could carry him, down the corridor, then through a nearby portal into training zone 6. He looked around for another way out but there was nowhere to go, and he could already hear Opo's footsteps coming after him. He spotted a storage zone and raced inside to hide.

"Kik-POP?" said Glitch.

"Shhhh!" said Hex, covering Glitch's verbalizer with a sucker. He held his breath and waited, but after a minute or so, he began to wonder whether Opo had given up and gone straight to Headmaster Sporg.

He had to get out of there without anyone noticing him. He looked around for something, anything that he could use to disguise himself. There were dozens of shelves, each filled with hundreds of containers, all clearly marked: RAY-GUNS, PULSE-GRENADES,

DEFLECTION SHIELDS, MAGNA-BOOTS... Everything a space invader in training could need. Suddenly, something caught his eye. A container marked HOLO-SUITS.

Hex shivered. He hadn't had much luck with holo-suits. In fact, Hex's one and only holo-suit experience had been probably the craziest hour of his life. Then again, he had ended up saving Earth from invasion. He knew it was his only chance. He lifted the crate down and took out a holo-suit. He gulped down a deep breath and put it on.

"POP! Chik POP!" said Glitch, anxiously.

"I know, but what other choice do I have?" replied Hex. He pulled the hood over his head and tugged the zip all the way up. The holo-suit flickered and Hex was transformed ... into a purple-skinned, ten-tentacled gwirm.

"POP! POP!" said Glitch in horror.

"Must have been left over from another invasion. This is no good, I can't go walking around as a gwirm, I'll be disintegrated on sight. If I could just recalibrate the imager somehow . . . where's the image modulizer?" said Hex. He reached under his armpits, then behind his knees, then on the soles of his feet. "Transponding nodules . . . phase array . . . diffusion circuits. . ." Finally, he inspected the tips of his suckers.

"There they are!" he cried. As Glitch looked on in disbelief, Hex clicked his suckers together, and the holo-suit image flickered and then changed! Within moments, Hex looked like a flat-tailed bundin.

"How do I look?" he said, looking down his long, scaly snout.

"Klik-ka-chik chik-ik!" said Glitch, shaking his head.

Hex clicked his suckers again, making him look like a many-headed mokkrul. Then again, disguising him as a blue-furred flox. Before long, the holo-suit had scrolled through twenty disguises, from aliens of every size and shape to a planetexian police officer. Eventually he clicked his way to an assisto-bot disguise. Hex looked down at his thin, metal pincers.

"An assisto-bot will do nicely! They're all over the school – no one will look twice at me. Come on, Glitch."

Glitch rolled on to Hex's shoulder as Hex opened the storage zone door carefully and sneaked out. His disguise was perfect – he even whirred and clanked as he moved! Now all he had to do was to get out of the school and as far away as possible.

Hex walked down corridor after corridor, past training zone after training zone, until he reached the ingestion zone. It was full of hungry children, all happily tucking into bowls of gloop. He spotted Dooper and Steek, but no Opo! Had she headed straight for Sporg's zone to tell him everything?

Hex fought every instinct to run, and slowly made his way through the ingestion zone. He was halfway to the door when Opo burst in behind him. She took one look at him and raced towards him! Hex was about to make a break for it, when she ran straight past.

"Dooper! Have you seen Hex?" she said, grabbing Dooper as he stuffed his feeding tube with gloop.

"Where's he gone now? I can't keep up with him!"

laughed Dooper. "He's always teleporting off somewhere or other. Maybe he's squeezing in some extra space invaser training!"

Hex didn't wait for Opo to tell Dooper his terrible secret. He headed straight for the exit . . . but in his panic he failed to notice a glob of spilled gloop directly in his path.

SWIII–IIP!

Hex's feet flew out from underneath him and he crashed to the floor! As he lay on the floor, dazed, Opo and Dooper (and almost everyone else in the ingestion zone) turned to see what had happened. Hex scrambled to his feet and started running.

"Ka-chik chik POP POP?" asked a concerned Glitch.

"Shhh!" replied Hex. "Keep quiet, or we're as good as disintegrated!"

"Hex?" said Opo, recognizing Hex's voice. She spun around and along with everyone else, saw an assisto-bot dashing away. Everyone stared as it clambered over a table and out into the main hall.

Only one pupil looked down at the floor where the

assisto-bot had slipped on gloop – *Steek*. He noticed something small and silver lying on the ground, and as he leaned down and picked it up, he realized that it was a P.A.D.

Steek turned it on and the P.A.D. pinged into life. He inspected it closely, wondering why an assisto-bot would have its own Personal Advice Device. Then, as he stared at the screen, Steek suddenly had his answer.

HEX? ARE YOU THERE, SON? WHAT'S GOING ON?
HAVE YOU BEEN FOUND OUT?

"Son?" said Steek. "I knew it . . . I knew it!"

HOW TO STEAL
A HYPERSAUCER

Hex ran on to the huge landing platform outside the school, and then dashed to a nearby elevation tube and darted inside. He was immediately whisked up to a magna-bridge high above the school.

By now, Hex's mind was racing far faster than he was. Who had Opo told? Dooper? Headmaster Sporg? Maybe the police, or the empress herself? Whoever she'd told, Hex had run out of time – he had to get off Planet X, *today*.

"Klick-chik-ka-chik?" asked Glitch.

"I don't know!" replied Hex, staring out of the window. "I don't know where I'm going. . ."

Hex raced across the bridge and hopped on to a fast-moving conveyor belt. He shuffled between the crowds of planetexians going about their business, until he was dwarfed on either side by the vast, gleaming towers of New X City.

Finally, exhausted, he spotted a magna-tram pulling into a nearby waiting platform. He jumped off the conveyor belt and hurried on to the tram just as the doors closed. He stared at the vid-screen above his seat, trying to look like any normal assisto-bot riding a magna-tram would. Advert after advert flashed up in front of his face.

**Come to GWOOP'S HOUSE OF GLOOP
for an all-you-can-eat Festival of Feeding!
Ingest away, for just
99 Quix 99!
Fill up and get fighting fit!
GWOOP'S HOUSE OF GLOOP.
All you can eat – because
it's all you can eat!**

GOOD NEWS!

UNSTOPPABLE SUPER SENTRY-BOT BODYGUARD FOR EMPRESS VALOONA 99% COMPLETE!

As the magna-tram sped through New X City, Hex realized he no longer had any idea where he was. He had travelled further than he had ever been . . . but he was no closer to having an escape plan. Then, as if on cue, an advert flashed up on the vid-screen in front of him.

This was the answer! Hex didn't need to steal a hypersaucer – he could buy one! All he needed was 9,999,999 quix! Hex reached into his pocket and searched around for his pocket money. He had never been very good at saving. He tended to spend everything he had on spare parts for his robot creations.

"Two quix and twenty-four voots," he said, staring at the six tiny coins in his sucker. Hex sighed and looked at Glitch. "Only nine million, nine-hundred and ninety-nine thousand, nine-hundred and ninety-seven quix and seventy-six voots to go."

"POP-chik-ik?" asked Glitch, hopefully.

"Not even if I save up for a thousand years," replied Hex with a sigh. "There's no way I'm going to get a hypersaucer, unless. . ." Hex remembered what his dad had told him about stealing a hypersaucer. It seemed impossible, and more than a little wrong, but then he *did* have his dad's permission . . . and it was better than being disintegrated. He had no choice – he was going to have to borrow one of Honest Zeeb's hypersaucers to get to Earth.

Hex waited for stop 2395 and hopped off the magna-tram. He followed the signs for the emporium until he caught sight of a large, dome-like building, surrounded by a vast, open forecourt. It was filled with hypersaucer after hypersaucer, thirty or more – all gleaming silver and polished so hard that Hex could see his reflection in the surface. The only problem was, no one was going to let a boy (or even a boy disguised as an assisto-bot) get close enough to a hypersaucer to fly it away. He ducked behind a hypersaucer and started clicking his suckers! In an instant, the holo-suit began shifting image again.

"Glitch, tell me when I get to something I can use," mumbled Hex as he clicked through alien after alien and robot after robot. Glitch inspected each camouflage, one after the other, and kept shaking his head. Finally, Glitch popped and nodded in excitement.

"This one? What is it? What do I look like?" asked Hex, and then caught his reflection in the hypersaucer's hull. He almost jumped out of his holo-suit. . .

He looked like Empress Valoona.

HONEST ZEEB'S HYPERSAUCER EMPORIUM

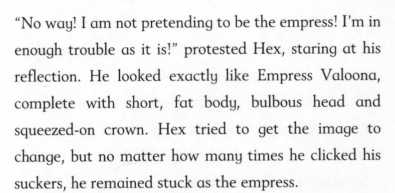

"No way! I am not pretending to be the empress! I'm in enough trouble as it is!" protested Hex, staring at his reflection. He looked exactly like Empress Valoona, complete with short, fat body, bulbous head and squeezed-on crown. Hex tried to get the image to change, but no matter how many times he clicked his suckers, he remained stuck as the empress.

"POP! Klik-ka-chik-POP!" said Glitch, approvingly.

"But I could get disintegrated!" began Hex. Glitch just stared at him. "Yeah, you're right . . . what's new?" Hex added. He sidled out from behind the hypersaucer and made his way towards the emporium entrance.

"OK, act natural," Hex whispered to himself, sneaking inside. "And . . . empress-like."

Hex crept into the emporium, trying not to be noticed by any of the other planetexians milling around. Hex spotted a short, fat planetexian behind a counter. He had a surprisingly small brain-sack and was talking into a hear-lobe-mounted communicator, so loudly that he could almost have been heard from outer space.

"Nah, listen, mate – I ain't talking about your run of the mill X7 or X8 model – no, no, no. I'm talking top of the range – the sort of saucer that turns heads and makes brain-sacks throb with jealousy. Your neighbours will turn red with envy when they see you pulling up in the X9! You want to know the long, short and green of it? You can't afford *not* to buy this hypersaucer! As true as the sky is pink – you need this hypersaucer in your life, or my name's not Honest Zeeb!"

"Uh, excuse me," said Hex, sheepishly, in his very best empress voice. Zeeb didn't even turn around – he just raised his sucker in the air and carried on talking into his communicator.

"Now listen, I've got an X9 in the lot right now – one careless owner, 456,000,000 light years on the clock, all the trimmings. . . Why don't you pop by today, give it a test-fly?"

"Um . . . I'd like to buy a hypersaucer, please," whispered Hex, even more timidly.

"I *said*, keep your antenna on – I ain't an eight-armed octolillo, I've only got the one set of suckers," said Zeeb, abruptly, still not bothering to look up.

Glitch shook his head and reached out a pincer, pinching the salesman hard on the hear lobe.

"YOW!" squealed Zeeb, spinning around. "Here, what on Planet X do you think you're—"

He froze.

"You're – you're – Your Majesty!" Zeeb squealed and immediately dropped to his knees. "Forgive me, Your Majestic Greenness, I didn't see you there! A thousand million billion apologies!"

"Uh, not to worry . . . no need to make a fuss," replied

Hex as everyone in the emporium turned to see what all the commotion was about. The second they laid eyes on the empress, they, too, fell to their knees! Hex tried not to smile. This might be easier than he'd thought. . .

"How can I be of service, Your Marvellous Majesticness? Would you like an emporium tourium? I mean, a pour of the emtorium? I mean, a *tour of the emporium*?" stumbled Zeeb. "Everything's above-board and green, of course! This is just a hobby really – something to do between space invasions! You know what it's like – got to make a living, got to feed the hatchlings. . ."

"Uh, I'd like – I mean, your empress would like a hypersaucer," said Hex, trying to sound empress-like. "The best one you've got."

"Of course! Take whichever one you want! Free of charge, of course! Everything you see belongs to you anyway, Your Empressness!" said Zeeb, guiding Hex outside to the hypersaucer lot. "How about this X-8500 – it's been through two invasions and flies like a dream! But what am I thinking? You want the best of the best!"

"Uh, yes, the best of the best would be . . . best," said

Hex, noticing a small crowd of onlookers and floating vid-bots starting to gather outside the emporium. The last thing he wanted was to appear on a news-vid!

"Nothing else would do for Her Megajestic Empress!" said Zeeb, continuing to bow as he directed Hex to the largest, most impressive looking hypersaucer in the lot. "The X10 – fresh from the invasion of this Planet X! Now I only have two of these, but you're welcome to them both!"

"This looks perfect!" said Hex, excitedly. "But can I just check . . . would this hypersaucer get me, or someone else, all the way to – oh, I don't know – Earth?"

"*Earth*, Your Majesty?" said Zeeb, suspiciously. "As in, *Planet* Earth?"

"Yes, yes, Planet Earth – the, uh, the stinking mudball that I was going to invade but then didn't – that one," said a nervous Hex, as the crowds outside grew larger. "I was just curious, you know, in case I fancied a holiday, or . . . a day trip, or something. . ."

"Well, no, of course not, Your Most Masterful Empressness," said Zeeb, as though he was being tested. "None of these hypersaucers can get off the planet – by your own royal command."

"Wh-what? What do mean, *none* of them?" asked Hex.

"Well, no. Every second-hand hypersaucer has its hyperdriver removed – just like you ordered, so it can't . . . I mean, so no one can. . ." began Zeeb, awkwardly.

". . .*escape*," finished Hex, suddenly realizing what Zeeb

meant. He looked around at the sea of hypersaucers. They were useless to him. They couldn't even get him into space, never mind all the way to Earth!

"Not that anyone would want to escape!" said Zeeb quickly. "Not when life as a planetexian is so glorious! All hail Your Majesty! All hail space invasion! If in doubt, disintegrate!"

"No, no, no. . ." said Hex, despairing. "You mean, you don't have *any* hypersaucers that can get me to Earth?"

"No offence, Your Most Majestic Empress, but don't you have a whole *fleet* of invasion-ready hypersaucers at your disposal – I mean, brand new ones, with hyperdrivers and everything?" said Zeeb, daring to inspect Hex a little more closely.

"What? Uh, yes, of course I do!" said Hex, panicking about blowing his cover. "Don't question the empress! Do you want to be disintegrated?"

"N-no, Your Majesty! No, I didn't mean anything! Forgive me, Your Majesty!" screamed Zeeb, throwing himself at Hex's feet, again.

"Yeah, well, OK then – just don't do it again," said

Hex. "Now, can you get a hypersaucer with a working hyperdriver or not?"

"Well, I might have the odd one..." said Zeeb, uneasily. "Not that I sell them, you understand! I just ... haven't got round to altering them. I mean, who'd want a hypersaucer that could go into space? Who'd want to leave Planet X? No one, that's who! Everyone loves it here!"

"But if I wanted to leave..." began Hex, cautiously.

"These babies would take you anywhere you wanted to go! Perfect for, uh, day trips," said Zeeb, looking a little suspicious. Hex straightened his holo-crown and tried to look regal.

"I'll take one," he said.

ESCAPE FROM PLANET X
(1ST ATTEMPT)

Zeeb led the disguised Hex through the emporium and into his office. He reached up to a picture of two plump planetexian children mounted on the wall, and slid it aside. Behind it was a large, green button. Zeeb pressed it and the wall split apart to reveal a secret elevation tube!

"This way, Your Most Wondrous Majesticness," said Zeeb, guiding Hex into the tube. Hex stepped nervously into the beam of anti-gravity, and slowly began to descend. Before long, the elevation tube deposited Hex and Zeeb in a huge, underground hangar. Hex took a sharp breath into his gills – it was full of hypersaucers, perhaps fifteen of them. They weren't polished or pretty, and many had blast marks and damage from previous invasions.

"Amazing. . ." said Hex, as he wandered into the hangar. "And they all have hyperdrivers? What are they used for?"

"Uh, well, the thing is. . ." Zeeb began awkwardly, his brain-sack dripping with nervous sweat. Hex remembered what Opo had told him, about there being *loads* of planetexians who didn't want to be space invaders. Suddenly, everything started to make a strange sort of sense.

"Do you sell these? Do other planetexians use them to escape?" continued Hex, sternly. "Your empress wants to know! I command you tell me! Has anyone ever escaped from Planet X?"

"They . . . they have tried. They come to me, wanting to buy space-worthy hypersaucers. . ." confessed Zeeb, hoping he wasn't sentencing himself to disintegration for selling illegal hypersaucers. "But no one's actually managed to escape, of course. Your hypersaucer fleet makes sure of that – they shoot down anything that tries!"

"Wait, so no one's escaped? No one *at all*?" asked Hex in horror.

"Of course not! Everyone knows you can't escape from Planet X! But people just keep trying – I suppose I'm selling a dream," replied Zeeb with a nervous laugh.

Hex felt rather strange. All this time he had thought he was the only creature on Planet X who didn't want to be a space invader . . . but Opo had been right all along – there were more. Hex wondered how many had tried and failed. Could his father really be the only planetexian who had ever managed to escape? Had it been the Hex Effect that had carried him through the black hole to safety? Might the same be true for Hex? After a moment, he took a deep breath and made up his mind.

"I'll take that one," he said, finally. "Don't bother wrapping it, I'll fly it out of here."

"Very good, Your Majesticness!" said Zeeb, delighted that he hadn't been sentenced to disintegration. He grabbed a set of keys from a hook on the wall and then waved them at the hypersaucer. With a *bip-bip!* the hypersaucer door opened and a ramp descended to the floor.

"Would you like to look around first? I could throw in some extras – no charge, of course! Air conditioning, suckers-free P.A.D. lock, fluffy dice. . ."

"No thanks, I'm in a bit of a rush, actually. Lots of empress stuff to do," said Hex. He was so close to escaping, he could almost smell the far reaches of orbit. He reached out for the key, but just as he was about to grab it, the image of the empress's fat sucker *flickered*. Hex quickly hid his sucker behind his back and looked up at a blinking Zeeb.

"You – yuh – wuh— " blurted Zeeb, staring at Hex, his mouth wide open and a disturbing look of surprise on his face.

"I'd, uh, I'd better be off then," said Hex, waving his sucker. "The work of a busy empress is never done . . . and that's me, the empress!"

It was then he spotted his sucker didn't look like a

sucker at all – not even a fat, empress's sucker – it looked like a tentacle! No, a scaly claw! No, a feathery wing! The holo-suit was going haywire!

"What . . . what on Planet X *are* you?" cried Zeeb.

"Well, goodbye then!" cried Hex, urgently! He tried to grab the key, but Zeeb held it above his head.

"You're not the empress!" he shouted, and grabbed Hex by the neck! There was a crunching sound as the holo-suit's image stabilizer fizzled and hissed, and a split-second later Hex looked like Hex again.

"You crafty nudlork, it's a holo-suit! You're just a little runt!" growled Zeeb, drawing a ray-gun from his tele-belt and pointing it in Hex's face.

"AAH! Wait! Please! It's . . . it's not what it looks like!" gasped Hex, as Zeeb tightened his sucker-grip.

"Chik-POP!" pleaded Glitch.

"I almost gave you my best hypersaucer! I . . . I kissed your feet! You filthy slipe! Don't you know it's a disintegrate-able offence to disguise yourself as the empress?" said Zeeb, pressing his ray-gun into Hex's face.

"Please . . . just . . . need . . . hypersaucer. . .!" gasped Hex, desperately.

"It's too late for that, you little skutchweed," snarled Zeeb. "Now you'd better be green with me: does anyone else know you're here?"

"No . . . no one at all . . . I promise!" cried Hex.

"Good, that'll make disintegrating you a whole lot easier. . ." Zeeb said, but as he was about to pull the ray-gun trigger, Glitch jumped off Hex's shoulder and on to Zeeb's brain-sack! He started rolling around his head, grabbing hold of whatever he could – antenna, hear lobes, even gills!

"Get off me!" shouted Zeeb, plucking Glitch off and throwing him across the hangar. Glitch bounced off a hypersaucer and fell motionless to the ground.

"Glitch!" cried Hex.

"Right, no more messing around!" boomed Zeeb. "Give my regards to the Little Green Man in the Sky. . ."

"Hey!" came a cry from behind Zeeb. Hex turned to see two figures rushing out of the bottom of the elevation tube. It was Opo and Dooper!

"Who on Planet X. . .? What is this, a school trip?" said Zeeb. He pointed his ray-gun straight at them . . . but Dooper had Hex's ray-gun. As Hex screamed "Get out of here! Run!", Zeeb and Dooper both fired.

ZWAAARK! ZWAAARK!

RAY-GUNS AND
REVELATIONS

The beam from Zeeb's ray-gun streaked across the hangar, singeing Dooper's antenna, but Dooper's own shot hit Zeeb squarely in the chest! He staggered backwards, his head spinning, and then slumped to the floor and immediately started snoring.

"Good shot, Dooper!" said Opo. "Still, he's only stunned – let's not hang around too long."

"What are you doing here?" asked Hex, panicking. "How did you find me?"

"Well, I thought I heard your voice back in the ingestion zone but I couldn't see you . . . then when I saw an assisto-bot I knew something wasn't right – Miss Voob told us they were all working on the empress's super sentry-bot. I realized you'd probably done something crazy . . . like disguised yourself with a holo-suit," replied Opo.

"It seemed like a good idea at the time," said Hex, looking down at the wrecked holo-suit.

"Well I decided to go after you, and Dooper agreed to help," said Opo.

"Well we *are* Team Dooper, Hex and Opo – BOOM!" bellowed Dooper.

"The hardest part was following you all the way here – we nearly lost you after you got off the magna-tram. But then I saw a news-vid of Empress Valoona trying to buy a hypersaucer from Honest Zeeb's Hypersaucer Emporium and sort of guessed it might be you – especially as the empress never leaves her palace," Opo said. "Then when we sneaked in and found the elevation tube, it all made sense."

"Team Dooper and Opo to the rescue!" said Dooper.

"Are you going to tell everyone about me?" asked Hex,

panicking. "Please, don't! I don't want to be disintegrated!"

"No! No, of course not! Why would we want to see you disintegrated?" replied Opo. "I told you, we're your *friends*. I mean, we *did* just save your life, you know. . ."

"Sorry, it's just . . . well, I thought if you knew what I'd done. . ." began Hex, picking up a dazed, slightly dented Glitch.

"Hex, I keep telling you – you're not the only planetexian who doesn't want to be a space invader. I hate it more than anything! But nobody talks about the downside, do they? Nobody talks about losing your family or moving around all the time or never being able to do anything that's not about blowing stuff up! Nobody talks about anything except how great space invading is," said Opo. "Well, I think it's amazing what you did – if I had the chance to save my mum like you saved your dad, I'd have done exactly the same thing."

"Wait a minute, *neither* of you want to be space

invasers? Really? Honestly at all? Not even a teeny little bit of a bit?" asked Dooper, a look of horror on his face.

"Sorry, Dooper. I didn't know how to tell you," said Hex. "I know how much space invading means to you – I mean, it's all you ever talk about. . ."

"But – but – but—" began Dooper. "But this is great! I thought I was the only one!"

"The only one. . . What?" asked Hex.

"The only planetexian who hated space invasing! I thought there was something wrong with me! Space invasing, space invasing, all the time! Why do you think I always shout about space invasing so much?"

"You don't want to be a space invader? Really?" said Hex, not quite believing what he was hearing.

"I hate it! I just *really* wanted to fit in. . ." replied Dooper. "Hey, we could form a new team! Team Dooper, Hex and Opo, the secretly-don't-want-to-be-space-invasers!"

Hex felt as though a weight was being lifted off his

brain-sack . . . and thoroughly guilty for not trusting his friends in the first place.

"I'm sorry I ran off like that," said Hex. "I thought if I could steal a hypersaucer I could get away before everyone found out what I'd done."

"Well, then, it looks like we found you just in time," said Opo. "Don't you know what happens to planetexians who try and escape?"

"Yeah, Honest Zeeb let me in on the secret," said Hex.

"Hex, the only way you're going to get disintegrated is if you get on that hypersaucer. Your secret is safe with us, right, Dooper?

"Right! We're Team Dooper, Hex and Opo!" hollered Dooper.

"Thanks. I appreciate it, I really do," said Hex, slipping the dazed Glitch into his pocket. "Now let's get out of here before Zeeb wakes up."

Hex ushered Opo and Dooper into the elevation tube and then hurried out of the emporium. By now, there were planetexians swarming all over the place, eager for a glimpse of their empress. Hex, Dooper and Opo slipped into the crowds and were soon on a magna-tram heading across New X City.

P.A.D. LUCK

As the magna-tram made its way through the city, the vid-screens were full of stories of the empress making her first ever appearance outside her emerald palace.

EMPRESS LEAVES PALACE FOR THE FIRST TIME!

o △

EMPRESS SEEN BUYING SECOND-HAND HYPERSAUCER!

o △

EMPRESS SAYS, "IT WASN'T ME! I'D NEVER MINGLE WITH COMMON FOLK!"

Opo giggled and prodded Hex in the ribs. Hex managed a smile, and had to admit that he felt better than he had even before starting space invader school. He may not have escaped from Planet X, but now he wasn't even sure that he wanted to leave. Finally, he knew there really were planetexians like him. He knew he wasn't alone.

Three conveyor belts and a skybus trip later, Hex was home. He waved to his friends as he hopped off the skybus, and they gave him the suckers-up. Hex walked through the portal with a broad grin on his face.

"Well, someone's had a good day! And you know what they say – a happy invader is a better invader," said his mother as Hex wandered cheerfully into the ingestion zone. "So, how was school?"

"Oh, you know Mum, same old, same old," said Hex.

"Well, did you hear about the empress? She was seen at a hypersaucer emporium, in the middle of New X City! Can you imagine?"

"No, I hadn't heard – too busy training, I suppose," smirked Hex. He gulped down a bowl of gloop and made his way to his zone. He took Glitch out of his pocket and made sure his robot didn't have any permanent damage.

"How are you feeling?" he said as he popped out a dent that was squashing Glitch's gyros.

"Klik-ka-chik POP!" said Glitch, with relief. He looked around and added, "Chik-kik-ka-chik-ik?"

"No, we're not in Zeep's hypersaucer emporium, or in outer space for that matter. I decided we might stay here for a while."

"Chik-POP! Clik-POP!"

"No, I just feel like maybe . . . maybe I have a reason to stay," Hex replied, staring out of his window at the three planetexian moons. "Speaking of which, I should probably break the news to Dad. . ."

Hex reached down to his tele-belt for his P.A.D. but

it wasn't there. He checked all round his tele-belt, then the floor, then every container, drawer, nook and cranny in his zone.

"Where is it? WHERE IS IT?" he shrieked in panic. "WHERE IS MY P.A.D.?!"

"Ka-chik POP! POP! POP!" said Glitch.

"How can I be calm? My dad is on that P.A.D.! What if I never find it? I'll never be able to speak to him again! Or worse, what if someone else finds it? I didn't delete Dad's messages! Everything he's ever sent me is still on there!" he cried, hysterically. "When did I last have it? I remember speaking to Dad in the corridor at school . . . but I've been all over the city since then! It could be *anywhere*!"

"POP! Chik! POP!" Glitch said, sternly.

"You're right. You're right, deep gill-breaths . . . I need to calm down," said Hex, pacing back and forth. "I mean, it's got to be *somewhere*, right? And why would anyone care about a lost P.A.D.? They probably wouldn't look at it twice. I have to retrace my steps. I have to find it, now!"

"Have to find what?" said his mother. She was standing in the doorway, her suckers on her hips.

"Mum! Hi! H-how long have you been listening? I mean, standing there?" asked Hex.

"Long enough," she said, sternly. "Now, you have 3.2 seconds to tell me *exactly* what's going on."

"I – I don't – uh . . . nothing," said Hex, but he knew it was too late. His mother had heard everything. She knew about his dad. His secret was well and truly out.

"Don't lie to me, Hex-37 – I heard what you were saying," she said. "You've lost your P.A.D., haven't you?"

"What? I mean, yeah, I did. . ." said Hex, quickly.

"Oh, Hex, what have I told you about looking after your things?" said his mother. "How can you expect to be a space invader if you can't take responsibility for your Personal Advice Device?"

She hadn't heard him talking about his dad! Hex grinned involuntarily.

"And you can wipe that smirk off your face," continued his mother. "It may not seem like a big deal

to you, but P.A.D.s don't grow on trees you know. That little machine is one of a kind!"

"You can say that again," murmured Hex.

"Well, it's much too late to go looking for it now, and it's bound to be at school somewhere. It's not like you've been wandering around New X City, now is it?" she said.

"No, Mum!" said Hex, crossing his suckers.

STEEK'S REVENGE

Despite managing to keep the truth about his misadventures from his mum, Hex didn't sleep a wink – he was too busy worrying about his lost P.A.D. He stared out of the window and thought about his dad, hundreds of light years away and no doubt worried sick. Before long, Hex had worried through the entire night and it was time for school. He dragged himself out of his slumber pod before T.K. had a chance to whisk him out with a pincer, and stared at his bowl of gloop until the skybus arrived. As he hopped on, he could already hear Dooper shouting his name.

"Hex! I saved you a seat! Team Dooper, Hex and Opo, reporting for duty!" bellowed Dooper from the back of the bus. Hex shuffled down and squeezed in next to his friend.

"Another great day of space invaser training! I can't wait to disintegrate stuff! BOOM!" said Dooper, and then gave him a wink and a nudge. "Yep! Space invasing! That's what I love! BOOM!"

"How are you doing, Hex?" asked Opo from the seat behind him.

"Terrible . . . I've lost my P.A.D.!" whispered Hex.

"Your P.A.D.?" said Dooper and Opo together. "But where did – how did – when did –"

"I forgot to delete my messages! If anyone finds my P.A.D., they'll discover everything!"

"What are you three whispering about?" said Steek, leaning over the chair in front of Hex with a grin on his face.

"Wh-what? Nothing!" said Hex, quickly.

"Mind your own business, Steek! Can't you just keep your antenna out of other people's conversations for once?" said Opo.

235

"Yeah, get lost, Stink," said Dooper.

"POP! POP!" said Glitch, joining in from Hex's pocket.

"I'm so sorry to interrupt – my mistake, do carry on," said Steek, politely, and sat back in his chair.

"What's he being so nice for?" whispered Hex. "Did he have a brain-sack transplant or something?"

"No idea. . ." said Opo, suspiciously.

Before long, the skybus landed outside the school and the pupils clambered eagerly off. For once, Hex pushed to the front of the queue, desperate to look for his P.A.D. before school started.

"OK, we'll split up," said Hex, as the children gathered in the main hall. "Opo, you search training zone 6 and the storage zone. Dooper, you look in the ingestion zone, and I'll search the corridors. If we don't find it before the first lesson, we'll start again at break. . ."

"I wouldn't bother, if I were you, said Steek, whispering into Hex's hear lobe. "You'll never find it."

Hex froze. "Never find what?" he asked, nervously.

"Why, your P.A.D., of course," said Steek, as the

doors of the main hall slid shut. "Oh, I'm sorry, was I listening in again?"

"My – my P.A.D.?" whimpered Hex, turning around to face Steek. "Why, have . . . have you seen it?"

"Did I forget to mention? I found it in the ingestion zone, in a puddle of gloop."

"You found it?" squealed Hex.

"And then I happened to look at all the messages in your inbox. And guess what? I was right all along. Daddy's *alive*. And that's not all I found out. You've been a busy boy, Hex. . ."

Hex took a sharp breath. Steek knew. He knew *everything*.

"Where . . . where is my P.A.D.?" he asked in a small, desperate voice, hoping he wasn't going to get the answer he was expecting.

"Oh, I'm afraid I've already given it to Headmaster Sporg," said Steek, with a grin.

Hex suddenly felt dizzy, and his brain-sack started to ache. He remembered the sensation immediately. His mind was being probed!

"HEX-37!" came the cry, so loudly that it almost shook the walls. The crowd of gathered children immediately parted. It was just like Hex's dream. Hex peered to the far end of the hall, to see Headmaster Sporg on his floating podium. He was wearing a minding module on his head.

"I didn't believe it at first," said Headmaster Sporg, holding up a small, silver object. "But when Steek came to me with your P.A.D., I had to find out for myself. Because you see, the mind never lies . . . and I've just read yours!"

"Please, I—" began Hex, his whole world crashing around him like a malfunctioning hypersaucer.

"SILENCE! Never has one planetexian committed so many disintegrate-able crimes! Communication with other planets! Stealing a hypersaucer! Attacking the city! Teleporting into the empress's palace! And, worst of all, blackmailing the empress into calling off the invasion of Earth!"

The schoolchildren gasped in unison, hardly able to believe their hear lobes.

"Well, Hex-37?" continued Headmaster Sporg. "What do you have to say for yourself?"

"I just wanted to help my dad. . ." whimpered a defeated Hex.

"SILENCE! I have no interest in hearing what you have to say for yourself ! I have just given the signal to alert the empress. I suspect she will want to disintegrate you personally!"

"Ha!" guffawed Steek, unable to contain his joy.

"Steek, you slimy, scum-gilled little gwirm!" growled Opo. "How *could* you?"

"SILENCE! You will be taken to the empress's palace – under the watchful eye of the authorities," Headmaster Sporg said, as the hall was bathed in the familiar blue light of a teleporter. The air shimmered around Hex and a second later, four planetexian police officers had teleported into the hall! The officers surrounded him, their ray-guns drawn.

"Hex-37, you're under arrest!" shouted the police captain.

"Please! Wait! I can explain. . ." began Hex, cowering in fear.

"SILENCE!" yelled Headmaster Sporg. "Oh, except you, officers! You carry on!"

"Hex-37, you are to be delivered to the palace of Her Majestic Green, the Empress Valoona XIII, for immediate disintegration!" said the police captain.

"I told you you'd end up getting disintegrated!" laughed Steek. Opo turned around and swung her sucker into his face.

BLAM!

"Oh, shut up, Steek!" she said, as he fell to the floor, clutching his jaw.

As the police officers guided Hex towards the exit, Dooper stepped forward and unclipped his ray-gun from his belt.

"Nobody move, or you're all going BOOM!"

"No, Dooper, don't!" yelled Hex, as Dooper strode towards the officers. They immediately started laughing.

"Pointing a ray-gun at a planetexian police officer is

a disintegrate-able offence, tubby," laughed the captain. "Do you want to join your friend as a pile of dust?"

The officers aimed their ray-guns at Dooper, but he didn't stop. He just kept walking straight towards them, his ray-gun pointed at them.

"Drop the gun, fatso! I mean it, that's an order!" shouted the captain, now a little nervous.

"Dooper, please, do as he says!" cried Opo.

"Last chance, kid – you can't take us all on. There are four of us, and only one of you," said the captain, sternly.

"I disintegrated fifty-eight target-bots in thirty-nine

seconds, and they were all firing back," said Dooper, proudly.

"Fifty-eight? Really? I've only ever managed fourteen – and that took a whole hour," mumbled the captain, his antenna glowing blue with terror. "Shoot him, men! Shoot him now!"

"Really, Captain? He's just some fat kid," said one of the officers.

"How many times – I have overactive elbow glands!" cried Dooper, and fired.

ZWAARK! ZWAARK! ZWAAARK! ZWAAAAAAARK!

"Huh . . . target-bots move *much* faster than people – that was easy!" said Dooper as all four officers fell to the floor, stunned!

"OK, now we're *really* in trouble," whispered Hex to Opo.

"Enough! I have never seen such un-invader-like behaviour in all my life!" screamed Headmaster Sporg, zooming towards Hex on his podium. "I'll deliver you to the empress myself – who knows, maybe she'll promote me to *super* headmaster, if there is such a job."

"Hey Sporg!" came a cry. Headmaster Sporg and Hex turned around to see Dooper, pointing his ray-gun.

"Don't you dare point that thing at me! It's one thing to shoot an officer of planetexian law, but I am a *teacher*!" shouted Headmaster Sporg. "Now, put down the ray-gun, this instant, or else I'll—"

"Boom," whispered Dooper, a wide grin spreading across his face.

ZWAAAAAARK!

THE SUPER
SENTRY-BOT

With a single stun-beam from Dooper's ray-gun, Headmaster Sporg fell to the floor, well and truly stunned. Dooper twirled the ray-gun around his sucker.

"I could get used to this . . . maybe there are some parts of space invading I *do* like," he said under his breath.

"Thanks, Dooper!" said Hex. "I'll take that!" he added, prising his P.A.D. from Headmaster Sporg's sucker.

HEX? HEX, ARE YOU THERE? WHAT'S GOING ON? I HAVEN'T BEEN ABLE TO REACH YOU FOR AGES – DID YOUR P.A.D. MALFUNCTION OR SOMETHING?

"Yeah, *or something*," said Hex. "Don't worry, I'll tell you later – on Earth, hopefully! I'm on my way, Dad!"

Hex and Dooper dashed down the hall and were quickly joined by Opo as they raced on to the landing platform outside.

"FREEZE!"

Hex looked up. A police skycar hovered in the air above them!

"ATTENTION, HEX-37. THIS IS THE PLANET X POLICE! YOU ARE UNDER ARREST! SURRENDER IMMEDIATELY SO THAT WE CAN TAKE YOU TO THE EMPRESS FOR DISINTEGRATION . . . OR BE DISINTEGRATED! YOU HAVE FIVE . . . NO, THREE SECONDS TO COMPLY!"

"We surrender! Please, don't shoot!" cried Hex, waving his suckers.

"Hey, Sergeant, does that look like an 'I surrender!'

wave or a 'get lost!' wave to you?" said the police skycar pilot.

"Hard to tell . . . he does have a 'please don't shoot' look on his face," said the sergeant, peering through his viewscreen. "Then again, he could be bluffing. You'd better double-check. . ."

"ATTENTION, HEX-37!" said the pilot through the loudspeaker. "ARE YOU DOING THE 'I SURRENDER' WAVE OR THE 'GET STUFFED' WAVE? WE'RE TRYING TO WORK OUT WHETHER TO DISINTEGRATE YOU OR NOT."

"What? No! I mean, yes! I mean, the first one!" screamed Hex.

"Not exactly a definitive response," said the sergeant. "Tell you what, let's disintegrate him just a bit. An arm or a leg or something. . ."

"Yes, sir!" said the pilot. He reached out a sucker for the DISINTEGRATE button, when a blue glow of teleportation energy appeared behind the police skycar. Something was teleporting in!

A moment later, a huge shape appeared on the

landing platform – and Hex saw immediately that it was much worse than the police. It was a robot – and it was *huge*. Hex recognized it from the news-vids.

The super sentry-bot!

"**STOP! THE TRAITOR IS MINE!**" boomed the super sentry-bot, swatting the police skycar out of the way with a massive pincer and sending it crashing to the ground!

"I think it's talking about you," whispered Dooper.

Hex stared up at the gargantuan robot hovered in the air above them. For a moment, Hex was lost in terrified admiration . . . until he noticed a panel on the robot's chest slide open to reveal a huge holo-screen. It began to flicker and a second later an image of Empress Valoona appeared.

"Uh-oh," said Hex.

"Well, well . . . Hex-37 – at last we meet!" squealed the empress, excitedly. "Although, we've met before, haven't we? When you invaded my emerald palace, disguised as an earthling!"

"Please . . . Your Majesty, I mean, Your Empressness,

I mean . . . I didn't mean to . . . it was the—" began Hex.

"So, what do think of my *super* sentry-bot? Pretty nifty, isn't he? Especially the in-built voice control and holo-screen – I can command my unstoppable robot guardian, from the comfort of my emerald living zone! I get to enjoy all the disintegration without ever even leaving the palace!" said the empress, proudly.

"That's great," said Hex, trying to be as polite as possible.

"I *know* it's great, and it was completed just in time to disintegrate you! Well, the instructions did say to charge its anti-matter battery overnight, but how much power is it going to need to get rid of one little boy?" cackled the empress. "Let's find out, shall we? Super sentry-bot, destroy him!"

"RUN! Find cover! It's me she's after!" shouted Hex as the super sentry-bot silently obeyed its controller, swinging a massive pincer! It smashed through the wall of the school, sending up screams of terror from the children inside. Opo and Dooper dashed across the landing platform and headed for the crashed skycar.

They ducked behind it just as the two police officers scrambled out and ran for their lives.

"Uh, do you think this is a good place to – wait, where's Hex?" asked Dooper, peering over the skycar. "He didn't follow us! That boom-bot is right on top of him! We have to help him!"

"I know, I know! I'm thinking!" replied Opo, banging the skycar with her clenched suckers. It was then she peered inside, and noticed the keys were still in the activation slot. . .

By running in another direction, Hex was now well and truly cornered by the super sentry-bot. He stared up in horror as the super sentry-bot loomed over him.

"There's nowhere to hide, traitor!" cried the empress. "I'm going to disintegrate you, piece by piece! No one makes a fool of Empress Valoona! No one!"

"Klik-POP?" said Glitch, poking his head out of Hex's pocket. He pointed at Hex's tele-belt, which had started to rumble and spark.

"Not again! What's *wrong* with this thing? I didn't set

it to receive! It's not even – uh oh," replied Hex, as he stared down the barrel of a death ray-cannon.

"Let this be a lesson to all those who would betray me!" screamed the empress.

ZWAAAAAARK!

"Missed! Where'd he go?" screeched the empress, as Hex de-materialized in a flash of blue light! He had teleported! A second later, the empress saw Hex re-materialize a few metres away. "Aha! There you are!"

ZWAAARK!

Another death ray shot out of the super sentry-bot's cannons, but Hex teleported again, re-materializing nearby.

"Stop doing that! I can't disintegrate you if you don't hold still!" hissed the empress.

"I'm not doing anything!" cried Hex. "It's this tele-belt! I—"

ZWARK! ZWAARK! ZWAAAARK!

Hex teleported again and again, avoiding death ray after death ray!

"HOLD STILL, TRAITOR!! YOUR EMPRESS

COMMANDS YOU TO HOLD STILL!" screamed the empress!

"It's the Hex Effect . . . I think it's trying to save me!" said Hex, re-materializing elsewhere on the landing platform. Then, just as he was beginning to think his dad might be right about trusting the Hex Effect, he teleported and re-materialized . . . in mid-air, hundreds of metres above the ground!

"Or maybe not," he muttered as he started to fall!

"Ha HA!" cried the empress as she watched Hex plummet! "Goodbye, traitor! You've sealed your own fate!"

"YAAAAAAAAAAH!" screamed Hex – and "POP! Chik! POP!" screamed Glitch – as they saw the ground coming towards them at high speed. Hex's short, eventful life flashed before his eyes, especially the really terrible bits, after he had started space invader school.

As he was about to hit the ground, he remembered thinking his dad must have been wrong after all about the Hex Effect, and wished more than ever that he'd had a chance to see him again.

KRUMP!

"Ow!" cried Hex. He'd landed on something, but it certainly wasn't the ground. He opened his eyes to find himself on the roof of a (fairly battered) police skycar! He'd been caught in mid-air! He peered through the skycar's domed glass roof to see Opo and Dooper.

"Hi, Hex!" cried Dooper, waving. "Look what we found!"

"What did – where did – how did—?" began Hex, pressing his suckers to the roof as hard as he could.

"Don't worry, Hex, you're in safe suckers!" said Opo. "I got top marks in hypersaucer training and this is much easier than that! Now, hang on tight – I'm getting you out of here!"

"WAAH! Keep it steady!" gasped Hex, as the skycar weaved between two towers.

"Wherever we're going, we'd better get there quick – I don't know how much longer he can hold on," said Dooper. "Hey, where *are* we going?" he asked.

"Zeeb's Hypersaucer Emporium," Opo replied. "We're getting Hex off Planet X!"

TAKING CONTROL

The skycar weaved between the city's gleaming spires, as Hex clung on to the roof for dear life.

"C-can we find a place to stop? I'm s-slipping!" screamed Hex from the roof, but then he turned around to see the super sentry-bot zooming after them! "Ignore me! Go faster! GO FASTER!"

"Fasten your seatclamp, Dooper – and hang on, Hex!" cried Opo and hit the accelerator as hard as she could. Hex pressed his suckers harder as the skycar dodged and weaved between buildings.

"Come back here! You can't escape! I *command* you

not to escape!" howled the empress, as the super sentry-bot pursued them through the city, swatting skycars out of the way in mid-air. "Bah! Enough of this chasing nonsense. Super sentry-bot, lock on death rays!"

As Hex clung on, he craned his neck to see the super sentry-bot, which had stopped in mid-air. For a moment, he thought the empress had given up, but then he saw a flash of green energy.

"It's firing! Dive!" he cried, but it was too late.

ZWAAARK!

The blast struck the back of the skycar, disintegrating its main engine! The skycar lurched and spun in mid-air. Hex's suckers slipped and he was flung through the air at a nearby building! He closed his eyes as he saw the wall rushing towards him. . .

THUD!

"Oof!" cried Hex. He got up, made sure he was still in one piece and looked around. His tele-belt had saved him again! He'd teleported into a small, dark space, surrounded by huge banks of machinery and circuits and a thick jungle of wires.

"Klik-POP?" asked Glitch, rolling out of Hex's pocket on to his shoulder.

"I don't know ... some kind of computing zone, maybe?" replied a confused Hex. "Look at all this tech! Six-way sensor modulizers, triple reinforced X-tanium coupling rods ... motherboard *and* fatherboard, even built-in Greentooth®! This is cutting edge robotics. What is this place?"

Hex noticed what looked like a rectangular viewscreen. He made his way over to it and looked out. They were still in the middle of New X City. It was then Hex noticed a smoking, battered-looking police skycar, which had landed roughly on top of a tall tower. Suddenly, everything made sense.

"Klik-POP?" asked Glitch.

"Yeah, I know *exactly* where we are," said Hex. "We're inside the super sentry-bot! The Hex Effect teleported us inside its head! Look, that's the robot's eye-screen! And there's the power cartridge ... data bubbles ... control module. . ."

"Chik-POP! POP?" shouted Glitch, excitedly.

"The control module! Glitch, you're right, I can take control from here!" said Hex. He prised a panel off the primary control module. "If I can just disconnect the empress's command feed. . ."

Hex dashed around the super sentry-bot's head, disconnecting wires, bypassing recognition chips, rerouting binary streams. . .

"Hey, my vid-link's going fuzzy!" screamed the empress from her emerald remote command pod, far away in the palace. "What's happening? Super sentry-bot, acknowledge! Super sentry-bot, are you listening to me?"

"It's working! I think . . . just a few more seconds to lock down the transfer. . ." said Hex, hurrying back to the primary control module.

"Who said that? I hear a voice! Who's there?" screeched the empress, her vid-link flickering to nothing. "It's that child, that monstrous child! He's trying to take control! Someone fetch my royal technicians!"

"Ka-chik POP!" said Glitch.

"Nearly – got it!" said Hex, grabbing hold of the

primary control module. "Sorry, Empress – I'm pulling the plug on you."

"What? Don't you dare, you little nudlork! This is my robot! Mine!" screeched the empress, helplessly. "Guards! Technicians! Do something! DO SOMETHiiiiiing. . .!"

And with that, the empress was gone and Hex was in command of the most powerful robot ever built.

"Klik ka-chik POP?" asked Glitch.

"Nah, you'll *always* be my number one bot, Glitch. . ." said Hex, staring out of the super sentry-bot's eye. "But I bet you can't do *this*."

Hex squeezed the control module and zoomed through the sky! He laughed as the super sentry-bot spun gracefully around two buildings. It was much more fun than flying a hypersaucer! Then, after a swoop and a dive, he headed straight for Opo and Dooper's crashed skycar.

"The robot's back to boom us!" screamed Dooper, as the super sentry-bot loomed behind them. "Go! Go! Go!"

"I can't!" shouted Opo, hitting the controls. "We've lost our main engine – we're not going anywhere!"

"Well, it was nice knowing you, Opo. Your brother, not so much," said Dooper, as the super sentry-bot reached out its massive pincers. . .

"Don't worry, guys, I've got you," said a booming voice over the super sentry-bot's speakers, as it grabbed hold of the car and lifted it into the air. "Just sit back, relax and enjoy the ride."

"What's going on? I thought we were boomed for sure!" bellowed Dooper, as the vid-screen on the super sentry-bot's chest panel flickered to reveal Hex's face.

"Hex! Is that – how did – are you *inside* that thing?" said Opo.

"Cool, isn't it?" chuckled Hex. "We can take on anything with this robot! But without a hyperdriver, it still can't get me off Planet X. You're right, Opo, we have to get to the hypersaucer emporium, and fast."

"You mean, *that* hypersaucer emporium?" asked

Dooper, peering out of the skycar window. There, far below in the city, was Honest Zeeb's.

Hex landed the super sentry-bot outside the emporium. He peered through the window with its massive, single eye, and spotted Honest Zeeb behind his counter.

"Excuse me, please may I borrow a hypersaucer?" he boomed over the speakers.

"WAAAAAAAH!" screamed Honest Zeeb, and hid under his desk!

"This is the coolest thing that's ever happened to anyone," said Dooper. "You have your very own unstoppable robot! You can do anything, and no one can stop you!"

It was at precisely that moment that the sky began to darken. Hex turned on the super sentry-bot's monitors to find an entire fleet of heavily armed, invasion-ready hypersaucers approaching from the horizon.

"Are – are we being invaded?" whispered Dooper.

Within seconds, the largest hypersaucer had floated

down to the ground in front of them. Its landing ramp slid open, and after a moment, a familiar figure stepped on to the parking lot.

"Hex-37, what on Planet X do you think you're doing?" came the cry.

"*Mum?*"

SUPER SENTRY-BOT VS MUM

"I *just* got off the holo-vid with Her Majestic Green, the Empress Valoona XIII," said Hex's mum, as she strode towards the giant sentry-bot. "She told me someone took control of her super sentry-bot, and that I should get it back."

"Mum, I—" began Hex, desperately trying to disconnect the vid-screen to hide his face.

"I haven't finished! The empress told me she'd sent her new robot to hunt down an enemy of Planet X . . . a traitor! She told me he'd taken control of her robot, and he must be stopped at all costs! Now, who do I know who's an expert at robotics?"

"Klik-ka-chik-klik. . ." said Glitch, and put his head in his pincers.

"You're inside that thing, aren't you?" asked Hex's mum, firmly.

"N-no?" whimpered Hex, cradling the skycar awkwardly.

"Don't lie to me, young man!" shouted Hex's mum. "You don't think I know my son well enough to know when he's gained control of a giant killer robot?"

"This is worse than being boomed!" whispered Dooper from the skycar. "Hex's mum is really strict. . ."

"Shhh! We'll get told off too!" replied Opo.

"Well, what do you have to say for yourself?" said Hex's mum, sternly.

"Sorry, Mum," mumbled Hex.

"Sorry? SORRY?!" screamed his mum. "You're the world's most wanted criminal! You've broken almost every law we have! What on Planet X were you thinking?"

"I – I wasn't thinking! I'm sorry, Mum, I'm really sorry! I just – I just didn't want to be a space invader. . ."

"Is this what all of this has been about? Because you don't want to be a space invader?" yelled his mum.

"Well, yeah, that and I had to save Dad," said Hex, quietly.

"Your father? What's he got to do with anything? Your father is lost in space!"

"He's not! He's on Earth! And he wants me to go to Earth, too!" yelled Hex.

"Earth? Planet Earth?!" said Hex's mum. "I've never heard such nonsense in my entire life. Now, come out of that giant killer robot at once!"

"But Mum, I can't! I'm escaping!" cried Hex.

"You're doing no such thing!" growled his mum. "Look around you, Hex – you're surrounded by an entire fleet of hypersaucers – how on Planet X are you planning to get past them, hmm?"

Hex bowed his head in despair. His mum was right – he'd blown it. He'd been caught, green-suckered, and there was nothing he could do.

Then he remembered he was in control of the most

powerful robot on Planet X. Hex put the skycar gently on the ground.

"You should probably find somewhere to hide," said Hex. "This might get a little bit messy."

"Why?" said Opo, as she and Dooper clambered out of the skycar. "What are you going to do?"

"I'm waiting! Are you coming out of there, or not?" asked Hex's mum, sternly.

Hex narrowed his eyes and gripped the primary control module tightly.

"Not a chance," he said, and flew the super sentry-bot straight at the hypersaucer fleet!

"Hex-37, don't you dare even think about – uh-oh," began Hex's mum. "Evasive manoeuvres!"

The fleet scattered, but the super sentry-bot, under Hex's control, was too fast for them. It headbutted two hypersaucers out of the way, before grabbing another out of the air. The robot held it like a frisbee, and then flung it at another hypersaucer! An almighty **KRuNG!!** filled the air, before both ships spiralled out of control and were sent crashing to the ground.

"I'm taking those hypersaucers out of your pocket money, Hex-37! And – and I'm stopping your pocket money, too!" yelled Hex's mum. "All hypersaucers, regroup! Green formation! Disable that robot, but don't destroy it . . . or I'll disintegrate you all myself !"

"POP! Ka-chik. . ." said Glitch.

"Actually, she's taking it better than I expected," said Hex, as a dozen hypersaucers zoomed towards him, their ray beams streaking forth. Hex activated the super sentry-bot's force field, reflecting the rays back at them! As more hypersaucers fell out off the sky, the bot stopped two mid-flight and held them like a pair of giant cymbals. It began crushing the advancing spaceships between them, or swatting them aside like they were pesky shriek-flies.

"That's it! I'm revoking your holo-vid privileges for a year! No, two! No, for ever!" yelled Hex's mum.

On the ground, Opo and Dooper watched in awe of their new friend, the unstoppable robot, from the cover of the hypersaucer emporium, until a large shadow loomed over them.

"You're not getting away from me this time, you little nudlorks," snarled a voice. They spun around to find Honest Zeeb, his suckers clenched. "You're going to pay for what you did. I'm going to bash you both into gloop!"

Dooper and Opo looked at each other . . . and then Dooper drew his ray-gun from his tele-belt.

"Stun or mutate?" he asked, his suckers hovering over the dial.

"Oh, mutate, *definitely*," smiled Opo.

"Now, hang on. . ." squeaked Zeeb. "Let's not get carried away, I was only joking! I love kids! Especially ones who try to steal my hypersaucers! Let's work something—"

"BOOM!" shouted Opo, and Dooper instantly fired! The beam hit Zeeb, who immediately sprouted a second head and yellow scales. Seconds later, he shrank down to the size of a magna-boot, grew a dozen new legs and scuttled off in horror!

"Yep, this is definitely better than space invaser training," chuckled Dooper.

Meanwhile, Hex's super sentry-bot had already

crushed, crunched or swatted two-thirds of the 101st hypersaucer fleet.

"I'm going to give you such a piece of my mind when I get you home!" shouted Hex's mum. "Enough's enough! You've had your fun, now surrender, we have you surrounded on all sides!"

"Mum's got a point, Glitch," said Hex, checking the anti-matter battery readings as the hypersaucers approached from every angle. "This robot may be unstoppable, but the empress didn't charge it – we're already down to fourteen per cent of our power! We have to finish this, and quickly."

"Klik-ka-chik POP?" asked Glitch.

"Actually, I was sort of hoping you'd think of something," said Hex, chewing nervously on a sucker.

"Ka-chik POP! Chik-ka-klik POP! Ka-chik?" said Glitch.

"Hey, that might just work! Hang on to something. . ." said Hex. As the hypersaucers closed in, Hex began to spin the super sentry-bot in the air! Faster and faster, until it was a blur of green and silver!

"What's he up to now?" said Hex's mum. "Third wave, keep moving! Box him in!"

"H-h-h-hold on, G-Glitch!" said Hex as the robot spun faster and faster. Hex crossed his suckers and then activated the super sentry-bot's shoulder cannons.

ZWAAARK! ZWAARK! ZWAARK! ZWAARK! ZWAARK! ZWAARK! ZWAAAAAARK!

Beams shot out in every direction, filling the sky! As much as the hypersaucers tried to dodge and weave, they couldn't avoid the barrage – every ship in a hundred-metre radius was blasted out of the air! Of the 101st hypersaucer fleet, only his mum's ship, far below on the hypersaucer forecourt, had been spared from destruction.

"We did it . . . we did it!" cried Hex. "And it's a good job too – that last trick cost us the rest of our power. We've got nothing left. . ."

"I am very disappointed in you, Hex-37," said Hex's mum, climbing back into her hypersaucer. She locked on to the super sentry-bot with her ray-cannons. "This is going to hurt me more than it hurts you."

ZWAAAAARK!

ESCAPE FROM PLANET X
(2ND ATTEMPT)

Hex's mum fired a single shot from her hypersaucer's ray-cannon. It hit the super sentry-bot with uncanny accuracy, knocking out its anti-gravity generator and guidance systems in one go. Hex and Glitch were thrown off balance as the "unstoppable" robot sank slowly, crashing through the roof of the hypersaucer emporium.

"Glitch! Are you OK? Where are you?" said Hex, scrabbling around in the dark of the super sentry-bot's head.

"Klik-ka-chik! Klik-POP!" replied Glitch, tangled in a mass of loose wires.

"Come on, we have to get out of here, Mum will be here any minute!" Hex said. "And I think I'd rather be disintegrated than face her after this."

As if on cue, the eye-screen of the super sentry-bot was shattered in a flash of death ray energy! Hex huddled in the darkness, fearing the worst, but when he finally opened his eyes, there was Dooper, blowing the smoke from the end of his ray-gun.

"Come on, Hex! Your mum's just landed and she doesn't look happy!" he said.

"You came back for me!" cried Hex.

"We never left – we were too busy watching you take down the entire hypersaucer fleet!" said Opo, proudly.

"I guess that was pretty cool," said Hex, blushing a deep green. He grabbed Glitch and scrambled out of the giant robot. Hex could already see his mum. She was out of her hypersaucer and striding across the forecourt towards them.

"Hex-37, you get back here right now!" yelled his mother. Hex didn't listen. He and his friends darted into

Honest Zeeb's office. Hex slid across the picture of the plump planetexian children, revealing the secret elevation tube. One anti-gravity ride later and Hex, Opo and Dooper were confronted with the sight of the twenty battle-worn hypersaucers.

"So, which one should I take?" asked Hex.

"Whichever one gets us out of here the fastest!" said Opo, grabbing a set of keys from the wall. She waved them around, and with a **bip-bip!** the ramp on the nearest hypersaucer slid open. The three of them stopped, staring at the open door.

"Well, I guess this is it, time to go," said Hex, looking down at his magna-boots. "Look, I, uh, I just want you to know, I really appreciate what you've both done for me, and – wait . . . did you say get 'whichever one gets *us* out'?"

"Well, of course – we're coming with you," said Opo.

"Yeah! We're the secretly-don't-want-to-be-space-invaders!" bellowed Dooper.

"That – that'd be great!" began Hex, but then shook his head. "Wait . . . if you come with me, I don't think you can ever come back. You'll never see anyone on Planet X ever again. And that's if we even make it out of here alive."

Opo and Dooper looked at each other. Then, after a long moment, they both grinned.

"Sounds good to me . . . and anyway, how would you cope without us?" said Opo.

"Team Dooper, Hex and Opo! BOOM!" bellowed Dooper.

"Ka-chik-POP!" huffed Glitch.

"Yeah, and Glitch," laughed Hex. "Sounds like a full hypersaucer crew to me!"

Team Dooper, Hex, Opo and Glitch hurried inside the hypersaucer. It looked just like the one Hex had piloted during his training, except a lot more dusty. He brushed the dust off the control panel and pressed the big green START button. He heard the hum of the engines and then de-clamped the moorings and wrapped his suckers around the controls.

"OK – here goes nothing. . ." he said.

"Young man, step away from that control panel this

instant!" said a stern voice. Hex spun around to see his mother, standing in the open doorway.

"Mum! I—" began Hex.

"Don't even bother trying to talk your way out of this, Hex. You've had your fun, but this silliness has to stop, right now!"

"It's not silliness!" cried Hex. "I don't want to be a space invader, Mum. I never have."

"Oh, Hex, that's nonsense – everyone wants to be a space invader," huffed Hex's mum.

"I don't! And neither does Opo, or Dooper, or probably *loads* of planetexians! Why do you think this place even exists? It's because we all want to leave. Everyone's hoping the next Planet X will be better than the last, but it never is! It's just the same . . . and it's never going to stop. Well, I've had enough! Just like Dad had enough. . ."

"Not this again! How many times do I have to tell you, your father is gone for ever, lost in space!" growled Hex's mother.

"But he isn't lost! He's living a new life, a life free of space invading, far away from here! And he's here, on my

P.A.D., because he looked for me – because he wants me to join him," said Hex. He held up his P.A.D. and turned it on. "Dad? It's me. I'm with Mum," said Hex.

"He's – he's really there?" said Hex's mum, suddenly looking a little emotional.

> **HELLO, VEXXA. IT'S ME.**

Hex's Mum took a sharp breath. "Hex-36? Is that really you?"

> **GOOD TO HEAR YOUR VOICE. I HAVEN'T SEEN YOU SINCE THE SOLAR ECLIPSE OF '98.**

"Oh, Hex-36 . . . that was the night you were lost in space," replied Hex's mum, putting a sucker over her circulatory organ.

> **I KNOW. I STILL THINK BACK TO THAT NIGHT. YOU LOOKED A RADIANT SHADE OF GREEN. I BET YOU HAVEN'T CHANGED A BIT.**

"You always were a sweet-talker. . ." said Hex's mum, a tear welling up in her eye. Then, suddenly, she shook her head and gritted her teeth. "Oh, no you don't! Don't think you can charm me, not after all these years – that was always your way out! You being alive doesn't change a thing! Do you realize how much trouble you've caused for Hex-37? What were you thinking, contacting him after all this time?"

> I SUPPOSE I WAS THINKING HE MIGHT NOT WANT TO BE A SPACE INVADER.

"And he was right, Mum," interrupted Hex. "I don't. None of us do."

"But don't you see? It's too late! I could usually pull some strings, but not after all this! The empress had already launched another hypersaucer fleet before I blew up the super sentry-bot – there's no way I can stop you from being disintegrated!"

"Yeah, I sort of thought that might be the case . . . sorry about that," said Hex.

"There's nothing I can do. . ." said Hex's mum, suddenly looking a little sad. "Except . . . except let you go."

"What?" asked Hex, Opo, Dooper and Hex's dad together. Even Glitch made a confused pop.

"Hex, I've dedicated my life to space invading. I've put it before my happiness, my marriage, even before you," confessed his mother, sadly. "Well, I may be a merciless conqueror of worlds, but I'm also your mum. I think I can put space invading second – for an hour or so. Now, all I can promise you is a head start – but I'm pretty sure that'll get you safely off Planet X."

"But what about the empress? Won't she want to come after us?" asked Hex.

"Not if she doesn't know you've left. As far as she's concerned, you could all have been disintegrated in the battle with my hypersaucers."

"Are – are you sure? I mean . . . I can go? And you're not disappointed in me?" said Hex. His mother just shook her head and gave him a hug.

"Hex, I think I always knew this would happen. You

may not be a born space invader – but you do have a lot of remarkable gifts . . . and you're very good at blowing things up, which has to count for something!" laughed his mum, but after a moment, she began to cry. She wiped a tear away with her sucker, and smiled a wide smile. "Now off you go, Hex, before I change my mind. Oh, and good luck."

And with that, Hex's mum walked down the hypersaucer ramp and waved a sucker as the door closed.

"That was close! I thought we were in so much trouble," said Dooper.

"Me too," said Opo.

ME TOO!

"Klik-POP!" said Glitch.

Hex just smiled, and then secretly wiped a tear away. He guided the hypersaucer out of the hangar. They zoomed down a long tunnel, finally emerging into the bright morning light. As they sped into the sky, Hex suddenly felt freer than he ever had . . . until he spotted a hundred hypersaucers hot on his tail.

"More of them! Your mum was right – it's a whole other fleet!" cried Opo. "Hex, turn on the hyperdriver, quick! Get us out of here!"

"It's still charging up – this thing hasn't been flown for years! I need ten more seconds!" said Hex.

"They'll have boomed us to pieces by then!" shouted Dooper.

At that very moment, Hex's mum raced into the parking lot. She looked into the sky, to see the hypersaucers race after Hex.

"UNAUTHORIZED LAUNCH IN SECTOR 5788," said the hypersaucer captain. "LOOKS LIKE AN ESCAPE ATTEMPT. PILOTS, LOCK ON TARGET AND PREPARE TO FIRE!"

"No!" shouted Hex's mum. "Hypersaucer fleet, this is Captain Vexxa! Let that ship go! It's just a decoy, probably piloted by remote control. The criminals have been . . . dealt with."

"ARE YOU SURE?" said the captain. "I HAVE BEEN GIVEN STRICT INSTRUCTIONS TO DISINTEGRATE ANYTHING EVEN SLIGHTLY SUSPICIOUS LOOKING. . ."

"I *said* let it go!" growled Hex's mum. "It's all over, Captain. They're gone . . . for ever. Now get back here, that's an *order*."

"UH, YES MA'AM. . ." said the captain.

"HYPERSAUCERS, BREAK OFF PURSUIT!"

"They're going away . . . they're leaving!" said Opo, watching the hypersaucers return to the city. "I don't get it. They had us dead in their sights. . ."

"Thanks, Mum," whispered Hex, as the hyperdriver reached full power. Hex pulled the big green lever and the hypersaucer shot through the atmosphere at faster-than-light speed, disappearing into hyperspace in the blink of an eye.

GREAT HEXPECTATIONS

After an hour or so of zooming through hyperspace, it became clear to Hex, Opo and Dooper that they were not being followed. His mum had kept her promise – they were free. Relieved, they sat back in the hypersaucer as they streaked across an unknown, star-filled wilderness. It stretched out endlessly in every direction, and seemed to all three of them to be a universe of possibilities.

"I like it out here. Everything's . . . less green," said a wide-eyed Dooper.

"Yeah . . . and Earth's out there somewhere. All we

have to do is find it," said Hex, and then looked down at his P.A.D. "We're on our way, Dad! The only thing is . . . how do we get to Earth?"

EASY! I'M PATCHING IN THE COORDINATES NOW, HEX. BASICALLY, JUST TAKE A LEFT AT THE ASTEROID BELT, RIGHT AT THE BIG STAR CLUSTER, AND THEN HEAD STRAIGHT FOR THE ENORMOUS, SCARY-LOOKING BLACK HOLE. . .

"Really? I mean, you're sure we're going to be OK?" asked Hex, turning left at the asteroid belt. "What if the whole flying into a black hole thing doesn't work the same way for us as it did for you?"

WHAT DO YOU MEAN?

"Klik-kik-ka-chik POP!" said Glitch.

"Exactly! What if, instead of being transported safely through the black hole and appearing somewhere sort of near Planet Earth, we just get lost for ever, or crushed to bits by massive gravitational forces?"

"Nobody said anything about losing or crushing!" said Dooper, nervously. "I'd rather be a space invaser than get lost and crushed!"

"Oh come on, Dooper – it's not like we ever really thought Hex knew what he was doing. . ." answered Opo.

"I'll take that as a compliment," said Hex with a shrug, veering right at the giant star cluster.

DON'T WORRY, EVERYONE. THE HEX EFFECT WILL GET YOU THROUGH, MARK MY WORDS. I'LL SEE YOU ON THE OTHER SIDE – ON EARTH! YOU'LL LOVE IT – I'LL PUT THE KETTLE ON, AND WE CAN ALL HAVE TEA AND BISCUITS WHEN YOU ARRIVE.

"Tee ant biskips? What's that?" asked Dooper.

IT'S LIKE GLOOP, EXCEPT COMPLETELY DIFFERENT! PLUS, IT ACTUALLY TASTES OF SOMETHING. YOU'LL LOVE IT!

"Better than gloop?" bellowed Dooper. "No way!"

HEH . . . I THINK YOU'RE ALL GOING TO LIKE IT HERE.
EARTHLINGS ARE GREAT – IF A LITTLE BIT WEIRD. AND DO
YOU KNOW WHAT THE BEST THING IS? IF YOU TELL AN
EARTHLING THAT YOU'RE AN ALIEN FROM ANOTHER PLANET,
THEY DON'T EVEN BELIEVE YOU! THEY DON'T EVEN THINK
ALIENS EXIST . . . WELL, MOST OF THEM.

"They sound a bit stupid," said Dooper, accidentally poking himself in the eye.

I'LL SEE YOU AND YOUR FRIENDS VERY SOON, SON. TRUST
IN THE HEX EFFECT – IT'LL BRING YOU HERE SAFE AND
SOUND, AND I'LL BE WAITING.

"Yeah, trust in the Hex Effect!" said Hex, almost believing it. As they peered at the viewscreen, the black hole loomed large before them. Hex guided the hypersaucer straight for it. "Hang on to your antennae, everyone – here we go!"

"Uh, Hex, you *do* know what you're doing, right?" whispered Opo, suddenly a little nervous.

"Of course! Don't worry – I have a feeling our luck is looking up!" said Hex. A moment later, the hypersaucer immediately began to rattle and shake, and the onboard computer immediately started shouting very loudly.

"ALERT! YOU ARE APPROACHING A BLACK HOLE! THIS IS A VERY BAD IDEA! PULL UP! CERTAIN DEATH INEVITABLE!"

"Or maybe not. . .!" muttered Hex. The hypersaucer felt as if it was about to fall apart! Hex, Opo, Dooper and Glitch grabbed on to whatever they could find, and prepared themselves for the worst as the hypersaucer was pulled towards the black hole.

"S-s-s-sorry I d-dragged you into th-this!" cried Hex, suddenly feeling less confident about his dad's plan as he felt his teeth shake in his head.

"N-n-no p-p-problem!" replied Opo. "Th-th-that's what f-f-f-friends are f-f-for!"

"T-t-team D-d-d-ooper, H-h-h-h-Hex and O-o-o- . . . oh, well you get the idea!" bellowed Dooper.

"K-k-k-klik-POP!" added Glitch.

By now, the black hole had engulfed them. The three planetexians (and one little robot) closed their eyes tightly as the hypersaucer disappeared into the void. The noise became deafening, as rivets and bolts popped out of the walls, and the whole saucer seemed to be crying out under the strain. Then, suddenly, there was silence. It was quieter than Hex had ever known.

Hex opened his eyes and tried to look out of the viewscreen, but it quickly became so bright that he had to look away, as if everywhere was filling up with stars. Hex closed his eyes again, as everything turned white. Then:

"ALERT! IMPACT IN 30 SECONDS! PULL UP! CERTAIN DEATH INEVITABLE – I MEAN IT THIS TIME!"

"What the – what's going on?" said Hex. A planet appeared in the viewscreen, and they were heading straight for it! Hex tried to pull the hypersaucer up for a proper landing, but it was too late.

"WHAT DID I TELL YOU? CERTAIN DEATH INEVITABLE!" screamed the onboard computer.

"That's really not helping! Hang on, everyone!" he cried, as the hypersaucer ploughed into the planet's surface! It skidded and bounced along the ground, driving through mounds of grey dust, before finally coming to a bumpy halt.

"We made it . . . we made it! Everyone OK?" asked Hex, counting his suckers.

"BOOM!" shouted Dooper. "That was cool!"

"We're in one piece . . . I can't believe it!" replied a shaken Opo.

"Klik-POP! Ka-chik!" said Glitch.

"Yeah, Glitch is right, we're only *just* in one piece," said Hex. "Looks like the hyperdriver's OK, but it's going to take a few hours to repair the guidance system. But we made it . . . we actually made it!" he cried, grabbing his P.A.D. "Dad, are you there? It worked! We're on Planet Earth!"

"Coordinates . . . 4581.09," said Hex, checking the controls, and then he peered out of the viewscreen at an endless grey desert. "There doesn't seem to be anyone around. Actually, there doesn't seem to be much of anything. It doesn't look quite like I imagined. It's just dust."

"Nothing, just space," said Hex, staring up. "Outer space, and stars, just the normal stuff. Oh, and a big blue planet in the distance."

I DON'T KNOW HOW TO TELL YOU THIS, SON, BUT I'M
AFRAID THAT BIG BLUE PLANET IS EARTH! YOU'RE ON THE
MOON . . . A FEW HUNDRED THOUSAND MILES
OFF TARGET.

"A few hundred thousand miles? Just my luck! Stupid
Hex Effect! What do we do now? The hyperdriver's
wrecked!" growled Hex.

"Does that mean we have to live here, now?" said
Dooper, sadly. "I was looking forward to tee ant
biskips. . ."

DON'T PANIC, SON, YOU'RE GOING TO BE FINE.
AND YOU'RE NEARLY HOME. . .

Hex clenched his suckers and took a deep gill-breath.

"Dad's right, we'll get there – I promise. We didn't
come this far to give up now," said Hex, inspecting the
hypersaucer controls.

He started rushing around the hypersaucer, making

adjustments. "I'm pretty sure we can take off using the thrusters. I just need to recalibrate the navi-module . . . divert power to the anti-matter chamber . . . reset launch coding . . . there!"

Hex's sucker hovered over the big green button. He stared out of the viewscreen again at the planet in the distance. Earth looked so close that he could reach out and touch it. What's more, it looked like *home*.

"Put the kettle on, Dad, we'll see you in a few days. . ." said Hex, and pressed the button. The hypersaucer chugged and groaned, and began to shake so hard it felt as if it was coming apart!

". . . With any luck!" added Hex – and crossed his suckers.

Look out for more by Guy Bass

Look out for more by Guy Bass